'You're *not* the girl I thought you were,' Tyler drawled, regarding her with a cold light in compelling dark eyes. 'It seems your independent streak doesn't extend to refusing a helping hand from more exalted quarters, for instance.'

It was a moment before the words and their meaning registered and then Venetia was suddenly, passionately angry. He leapt to all the wrong conclusions about her without cause, too stupid and too sure of himself to wonder if he could be mistaken or to give her the benefit of any doubt. How dared he make such a blatant attack on her professional integrity?

It was even worse than assuming her to be her man-mad sister!

Lynne Collins has written many Medical Romances based on personal experience of hospital life, backed by research and information from her many friends in the medical profession. She likes writing about hospital settings, with their wealth of human interest.

Married with one son and now living on the Essex coast, Lynne enjoys travel, meeting people, talking, walking and gardening.

Previous Titles

REPENTANT ANGEL
BEAT OF THE HEART
STAR SURGEON

HEART IN CRISIS

BY

LYNNE COLLINS

MILLS & BOON LIMITED
ETON HOUSE   18–24 PARADISE ROAD
RICHMOND   SURREY   TW9 1SR

First published in Great Britain 1991
by Mills & Boon Limited

© Lynne Collins 1991

Australian copyright 1991
Philippine copyright 1991
This edition 1991

ISBN 0 263 77415 5

Set in 10 on 12 pt Linotron Times
03-9110-52874
Typeset in Great Britain by Centracet, Cambridge
Made and printed in Great Britain

CHAPTER ONE

HEAD and heart filled with dreams, shapely figure disguised by the voluminous theatre gown and softly curling blonde hair bundled into a mob cap, Venetia busily soaped hands and slender forearms beneath a flow of running water that muffled the sound of approaching footsteps in the scrub annexe. It was her first day at the Alexander Memorial Hospital, and the dreams that dwelt in violet eyes with their sweep of long, gold-tipped lashes were not of some man who held the key to a heaven here on earth but of her future as a very junior registrar with the cardiac surgery unit.

Deep in thought as she scrubbed, elated but a little apprehensive too, she was startled out of her reverie by the unexpected appearance at her side of a tall, powerfully built stranger with a shock of jet-black curls, tanned good looks and broad shoulders that strained the seams of the V-necked tunic he wore over loose-fitting theatre trousers. The dawn of a slightly shy smile faded as Venetia failed to recognise him.

He glanced, nodded an absent greeting. Then, as he turned the taps of an adjoining basin, he did a double-take, belatedly registering the welcome familiarity of an oval face and dreamy eyes and a very kissable mouth.

'Hello!' he exclaimed in astonished, delighted recognition. 'I didn't expect to see *you* here—or again so soon!' His smile deepened and his dark eyes twinkled at her with a meaningful warmth. 'How *are* you this morning?'

'I'm fine, thanks.'

Venetia's tone was cool, rather crisp, for she had no recollection of a previous encounter and knew she couldn't have forgotten such charismatic good looks— or his obvious conviction of their impact.

A too-confident charmer with a glib tongue, she decided, determined to discourage the glow of admiring interest in the deep-set dark eyes. She had seen that particular look many times during the years of struggling through medical school and walking the wards and working like a demon to secure her present post with Rogan Linnie's surgical firm. During her years at the Marlborough on the other side of the city, she had been too involved with her work for flirtation, and she didn't expect things to be any different here at Sandy's.

So it was as well to snub overtures at the start.

Tyler Petrie dipped his dark head to look into the coolly averted face, a quizzical gleam in his smiling eyes. 'Giving me the brush-off? What did I do to deserve that, I wonder? You weren't so unfriendly last night,' he reminded her softly, taking advantage of the fact that they were temporarily alone in the annexe.

Venetia stiffened. 'I'm afraid you've mistaken me. . .' the chilly words were smothered by the warm, seeking pressure of firm lips, and strong arms pulled her close to a lean, muscular frame for a heart-stopping moment '. . .for someone else!' she finished on a gasp of outrage, thrusting him away. 'And now I shall have to scrub all over again!'

He laughed, a low, confident and totally unrepentant

chuckle. 'I never forget a face—and yours is really one to remember,' he told her warmly. 'I know it was a pretty wild party, but I wasn't so tanked up that I can't remember the girl I took home—or what came after,' he added with a soft, mischievous implication that brought a blush to her cheeks.

Indignation blazed in the violet eyes. 'I'm *not* the girl you took home, however,' she assured him icily. 'I never saw you before in my life, and I'm not in the habit of going to parties, wild or otherwise!' Angrier than a case of mistaken identity really justified, Venetia scrubbed fiercely at slim hands made unsterile by contact with that very powerful chest.

Tyler Petrie shook his head at her in amused reproach. 'I don't know what game you're playing,' he said in wry resignation. 'But you've lost me.'

'I certainly hope so!' On the tart words, Venetia snatched a sterile towel from the neat pile beside the basins and stalked to the far end of the annexe, annoyed with herself for recalling so vividly the taste and the feel of that warm, surprisingly sweet mouth and the startling leap of her body's involuntary reaction to his maleness.

She fought an unwelcome stir of physical attraction for a stranger. Men and medicine didn't mix, and she had no intention of being swayed from that conviction by an attractive smile and the potent sexuality that probably swept other women off their feet—and one in particular on the previous evening, apparently.

There was little satisfaction for Venetia in knowing just how the confusion of identity had come about!

Puzzled, Tyler began the familiar ritual of scrubbing for surgery, his dark eyes narrowing as they rested on the girl who tossed the used towel into a bin, dusted her hands with talc and eased them into skin-tight surgical gloves with a practised air. She was ignoring him now, but he was sensitive to the tightly coiled tension of her slight frame and rebuffed by the obstinate turn of her lovely head.

He wondered why she hadn't mentioned that she worked in Theatre when he had told her that he was a surgeon at Sandy's. Surely it would have been a natural exchange of information?

He knew most of the CSU nurses, but he had been away for some weeks and there had been staff changes in his absence. Many of the girls at Trevor's party had been Sandy's nurses, and he'd made a beeline for the prettiest. Now, encountering her again so unexpectedly, Tyler compared her offhand attitude with the warm encouragement of the previous evening, with some disappointment.

She really did seem to be a different girl this morning, but that might be expediency rather than the brush-off it seemed. A nurse who valued her job took care not to be seen flirting with a doctor or surgeon she met on the wards or in Theatre or Outpatients. This particular nurse, so pretty and obviously popular, was sure to be carefully watched by a notoriously strict theatre sister and she probably felt it would be wise not to seem on too friendly terms with him while on duty.

It had probably been foolish to kiss her in full view of any passing senior nurse or newly arrived colleague, but the challenge of an unexpected rebuff had gone to his head. The quickening of soft lips and the sensed quiver of delight in the shapely body had been the reassurance that Tyler sought. Later, they would probably laugh together over her pretence of indignation and indifference, and she would make up for both by going out with him that evening.

In the meantime, the demands of his job meant that he would have little time to ponder her apparent change of heart. Even without the usual quota of emergencies, his first day back at Sandy's promised to be a full one.

'Well, here's a couple of early birds, anyway.' Rogan Linnie, professor of surgery and consultant in charge of Sandy's CSU, strolled into the scrub annexe, a smile warming the harsh but distinctive features that were familiar to millions through the media of press and television. A successful pioneer of new techniques, a clever and dedicated surgeon as well as a very eligible bachelor, he seemed unaware of the admiration and the feminine ploys to attract his interest practised by some of the women he met in the course of his work. 'I'm delighted to see you setting such a good example, Venetia. Keen by name and by nature, apparently,' he added approvingly with a special smile for the girl he had known for most of her life.

'It *is* my first day,' she reminded him with a sparkling smile. 'I'm determined to make a good impression, you see!'

'Once you've found your feet we shall discover all your bad habits, no doubt,' he suggested with a twinkle in warm grey eyes. He nodded to his senior registrar, who regarded them with the surprised arc of a dark eyebrow. 'Good to have you back with us, Tyler. How was your Australian trip? I thought we might lose you entirely, but perhaps the women of Oz weren't to your liking?'

Tyler smiled, used to the badinage of colleagues who liked to exaggerate his success with the opposite sex. 'They certainly can't compare with a Sandy's nurse,' he returned lightly, slanting a meaningful glance at the gowned girl who had turned away to greet Rogan's anaesthetist.

Venetia Keen. *Ven* and not Van, then, presumably, he mused, realising he had misheard the name being bandied about by her friends at that party before he swept her off to a quiet corner. She probably didn't know his second name either. Instant attraction and its inevitable outcome had left little time for the nicety of introductions.

As she talked to Howard Wylie, he saw the sweet warmth of the smile that lightened the rather grave face with a luminous loveliness, the same smile that had caught his eye across a crowded room and sent him scurrying to her side.

Tyler felt a shaft of renewed interest in the girl whose superb shape was presently concealed by the folds of her green theatre gown but had been displayed to advantage by the low-cut, short-skirted black dress of the previous evening. At that party, he had felt the powerful and quite irresistible force of an attraction that he had expected to be as short-lived as all the rest. Now, meeting the gorgeous Venetia Keen again in very different circumstances and surroundings, he found himself thinking seriously of a more lasting affair.

'I expect you're nervous,' Howard suggested kindly. 'First day and all that. But none of us bites, I promise.

Except Tyler, perhaps,' he grinned. 'I take it you've met the professor's right-hand man?'

'Is that who he is?' Smiling at the friendly young man whom she had met and liked on a previous visit to Sandy's, Venetia pointedly turned her shoulder on the tall surgeon whose lingering gaze was as unwelcome and as offensive as his uninvited kiss.

Arrogantly sure of himself, he had made a stupid mistake, and now added insult to injury with the blatant admiration that was no compliment when he had confused her so absurdly with someone else!

'Senior registrar, very able and very popular, particularly with the ladies. Terrific bedside manner—and I'm not talking about the patients!' Very blue eyes twinkled at Venetia as he warned, 'He'll make a pass. You're a newcomer and you're pretty, and it's a combination he can't resist. But you'll be much safer going out with me.'

Venetia laughed. 'I'm sure I would, but I'm afraid I'll be much too busy with my work in the Unit and studying for my Fellowship to have time for dating anyone,' she said firmly, making it plain from the outset that she was nothing like her flirtatious sister except in looks.

She had been doubtful about working at the same hospital as Vanessa, but the chance of a place on Rogan Linnie's firm had swept aside her doubts. She was a good surgeon and she hoped to become a consultant eventually, with the help and guidance of the man who owed so much of his own success to her famous father.

While her sister had chosen nursing merely to fill the gap between schooldays and the brilliant marriage that she planned for herself, Venetia had always wanted to be a surgeon, in spite of the years of hard work and study that left little time or energy for anything else. Unlike the romantic Vanessa, she had never dreamed about falling in love and getting married. She wasn't frigid, as some people unkindly suggested. She was simply singlemindedly in pursuit of a dream.

Actually being *here*, gowned and gloved to take her place as a member of Rogan's team, was fulfilment of part of that dream, and as she adjusted her mask over her nose and mouth she felt very grateful to the man who had given her the job on merit and not because of any sentimental attachment. She meant to put her heart and soul into her future at Sandy's.

She wished she weren't the only woman on the firm, however. There were still too few of her sex who chose surgery, with its demands on stamina and personal life. She had met with some prejudice from male colleagues at the Marlborough and she hoped Sandy's surgeons were more enlightened. Fortunately, Rogan was an old friend and Howard Wylie looked like being a new one, and she felt she could probably work in happy accord with the others.

Except, perhaps, for the senior registrar, who was much too conscious of his good looks and physical magnetism and infuriatingly sure that he had only to smile or murmur some foolish flattery in that deep velvet voice for any woman he fancied to fall into his arms.

Just as Vanessa apparently had.

Well, her impulsive and sometimes very silly sister was welcome to someone so arrogant and so stupid that he couldn't distinguish between two very different women, she thought dismissively, turning her attention to Rogan, who was outlining the proposed procedure.

He swung round to her with an encouraging smile. 'I know you're familiar with this technique, Venetia, so show us what you can do. Open up the chest wall and prepare the site for a length of new artery.'

Having hoped for a few days of settling in to her new job before she was called upon to actually assist, Venetia was slightly disconcerted. Rogan might have faith in her ability and his own judgement, but there were plenty of people who disapproved of female surgeons, and she suspected that his senior registrar was one of them, seeing the powerful frame stiffen and the proud head turn abruptly in her direction.

Playing for time, trying not to panic, she turned to the anaesthetist, who was possibly the most important person in the theatre, being responsible for monitoring the unconscious patient throughout surgery and noting the first signs of any cardiac or respiratory distress. 'Is the patient ready, Mr Wylie?' The brisk formality was meant to disguise the flutter of her heart and the tightening knot in her stomach.

Howard made a last-minute adjustment to a valve. Then he nodded. 'Yes, he's nicely under. You can go ahead.'

Drawing a deep breath, she squared her slim shoulders and flexed her hands in the thin rubber gloves. This was the testing time. This was the moment when she began to show the doubters that a woman could make it to the top as a cardiac surgeon. Nothing was going to get in her way—least of all the unnerving bore of a pair of glinting dark eyes, although, as she briefly encountered their gaze, she was instantly and irritatingly reminded of the impress of a lean and potently male body that had taken her senses by surprise.

Dismissing the man and his intrusive magnetism, Venetia turned to the scrub nurse whose hand hovered above an array of gleaming instruments. 'Scalpel, please, Sister.'

Tyler Petrie stared in disbelief as she took the scalpel and made the first incision with a sure stroke to an approving nod from Professor Linnie. It had seemed an odd sort of joke, but he had been ready to laugh with the rest. Now he realised that both the Professor and the girl were in earnest, and he hastily revised his initial impressions of the beautiful Venetia Keen. For she was obviously not a theatre nurse, as he had assumed, but the new junior registrar who had been appointed while he was in Australia.

He recalled the rumour that the Professor had had a woman in mind for the job. A woman and a half, in fact, he thought admiringly, as slim hands separated bone and tissue and muscle, clamped arteries and inserted a succession of retractors with a deftness that many of her male colleagues might envy.

She wasn't just a lovely face and a superb body and a warmly responsive bundle of feminine fun in off-duty moments. She was also a clever, competent surgeon who commanded respect as well as admiration. As he assisted, obeying her soft-voiced but incisive instructions to keep a firm grip on a retractor or to irrigate the cavity, Tyler was suddenly convinced that he had finally met his destiny.

Good-looking and ardently sensual, he had a reputation as a heartbreaker, not entirely undeserved. But deep down, like most men, he was looking for someone to love, to share his life, to make success in his chosen career all the more worthwhile. He had found that it wasn't easy for a hard-working and ambitious surgeon to sustain a meaningful relationship with any woman, and it could be even more difficult if they were both in the same profession. Off-duty times seldom coincided, and dates were often broken or cut short by the demands of their respective jobs. A number of promising affairs had fizzled out in the past as a result, but he felt that he was prepared to make a very special effort to hold on to this new girl in his life.

The discovery of her true status had solved the problem of her earlier attitude, relieving his mind. For she obviously took her work just as seriously as she ought, and she had resented being treated as a man's plaything at a time when she was getting ready to do the traditional man's job of curing disease and improving the quality of life with scalpel and suture.

Tyler warmed to her sense of fitness. She was a girl after his own heart, indeed.

'Well done!' he applauded warmly, following her into the annexe and pulling his gown from broad shoulders. 'I had no idea that you were a rival for the consultancy.' His smiling words weren't entirely teasing, for it was obvious that this clever girl had a future as a Sandy's surgeon.

'Please don't patronise me,' Venetia glowered, the staggering charm of his smile failing in its probably calculated impact. She was tense, a little tired, from operating under the strain of needing to impress her new colleagues. 'No doubt you think that women were created merely for your pleasure, but we can do a man's job just as well as he can—and sometimes even better!'

Tyler held up crossed arms in laughing protection. 'Heaven save me from a feminist! I'm sorry, Ven, I didn't mean to tread on your toes.'

'And I'd rather you didn't call me Ven,' she snapped, rather unreasonably but resenting the easy familiarity that assumed they were already friends.

'Sorry,' he said again, smiling into her stormy eyes with warm understanding of the pressures that led to such irritability. 'Isn't that what your friends call you?' He was remembering last night's party and the laughing exchanges between a lovely, sparkling girl and her companions. Now those incredible eyes spat fire as she tugged impatiently at the strings of her gown. 'Here, let me help.'

Venetia jerked from the disturbingly intimate touch of the hands that brushed the nape of her neck. 'My *friends* know better,' she said tartly. 'And I'm quite capable of untying my own strings, thanks.' Finally mastering the tangle of knots, she tore off the stained gown and dumped it in a bin before stalking from the annexe to catch up with Rogan, heading for the surgeons' rest-room at the end of the corridor. He turned with a smile as she called his name in her lilting voice. 'That wasn't fair,' she challenged brightly as she reached him. 'You let me do most of the work!'

'And you did it just as well as expected,' he assured her, putting a friendly arm about her shoulders. Her part in the procedure had been straightforward assistance for a surgeon with her amount of theatre experience, but he had been impressed by her confidence. 'You're going to be an asset to the Unit, Venetia.'

'I owe you the chance to prove it!' Impulsively, she clasped the hand that curved about her shoulder and sent him a smile that brimmed over with affection and gratitude.

'Nonsense! You're a very clever girl, and you deserve to get on after all the hard work you put in at the Marlborough.' Rogan's arm fell away from her as he ushered her into the room where the surgeons congregated between procedures to drink coffee and talk shop or simply to relax.

Howard Wylie got up from a comfortable chair to offer it to Venetia, and she accepted with a smile. She neither wanted nor expected preferential treatment because she was a woman, but there was no reason why the common courtesies shouldn't be observed and appreciated, she felt.

When Tyler walked into the room some moments later, Rogan was pouring steaming coffee into cups, and he turned to hand one to his senior registrar with the easy manner that endeared him to his colleagues and made him a prime target for the fantasies of junior nurses. 'I've just been telling Venetia that she's made an excellent beginning,' he said lightly. 'She's obviously a chip off the old block. But perhaps you don't remember her father, Tyler? Sir Laurence was one of the pioneers of open-heart surgery, as you probably know, and responsible for founding this CSU.'

'Before my time. I'm afraid I never met the man. I'm familiar with many of his procedures, of course.' The sensual mouth tightened fractionally as Tyler glanced at the girl who responded to Howard Wylie's overtures with a warmth that contrasted sharply to the chill of her attitude to himself. 'I wasn't aware of the connection. So she's following in Daddy's footsteps. With a little help from her friends.' Smarting from a second rebuff, he wondered drily if Venetia Keen had vetted and discounted *his* degree of usefulness to an ambitious newcomer.

Rogan smiled at the sardonic tone. 'She applied for the post with all the right qualifications and some splendid references from the Marlborough. Should I have turned her down because her father was an old friend? In any case, I wasn't the only member of the interviewing panel,' he pointed out mildly. 'Venetia won the job on merit and there was no need for me to pull any strings on her behalf. She has the makings of a really fine surgeon—as you saw for yourself this morning.'

'Very impressive,' Tyler agreed. 'She certainly seems to know what she's doing and where she's going—and just how to go about getting there. I'll take that across to her, shall I?' He whisked another cup of coffee from Rogan's hand and strolled towards Venetia, a distaste in his dark eyes for the suspect closeness between consultant and new junior registrar that he had witnessed out in the corridor.

Perhaps that was the real reason for her sudden cooling, her reluctance to recall the undeniably mutual attraction of the previous night, he thought drily. Perhaps she hoped to succeed where a number of other women had reputedly failed in a bid for the heart of the distinguished Professor. Linnie was a cold-blooded operating machine with little or no interest in women—or so Tyler would have sworn until a few moments ago. Now he regarded his boss as a possible rival for a woman he found himself wanting with all the force of a deeply passionate nature.

Venetia looked up in slight surprise as the unsmiling surgeon thrust the coffee towards her without ceremony. 'Thanks very much.'

'You're *not* the girl I thought you were,' he drawled, regarding her with a cold light in compelling dark eyes. 'It seems that your independent streak doesn't extend to refusing a helping hand from more exalted quarters, for instance.'

It was a moment before the words and their meaning registered, and then she was suddenly, passionately angry. He was detestable—quite insufferable! Rude, arrogant, chauvinistic, prejudiced. . .words failed her! He leapt to all the wrong conclusions about her without cause, too stupid and too sure of himself to wonder if he could be mistaken or to give her the benefit of any doubt. How dared he make such a blatant attack on her professional integrity?

It was even worse than assuming her to be her man-mad sister!

CHAPTER TWO

SUCH an old-fashioned attitude in a new colleague was disappointing as well as infuriating, but Venetia was well aware that Rogan's senior registrar couldn't be the only person at Sandy's to believe she had won the job with the CSU through favouritism—or feminine persuasion.

Inwardly fuming, she smiled sweetly at the surgeon, refusing to let him see that he had drawn blood with the scathing attack and wondering what Rogan could have said to him to bring it about.

'We all have our own methods of getting what we want—and I can't say that I approve of *your* tactics, if we're indulging in some straight talking,' she said silkily, her violet eyes locking with the condemnation in the dark, scowling gaze. 'Frankly, you lack finesse.'

The barb was unmistakable in its implication, and it obviously hit home, for Tyler's handsome face darkened and he turned on his heel and walked away. Venetia looked at the powerful back, so expressive of the offence that a man who saw himself as irresistible to women *would* take at the pointed words, and smiled with satisfaction. That would teach him to cross swords—or scalpels—with her!

Howard whistled softly. 'I don't want to speak out of turn and get my face slapped too, but he can be a powerful enemy,' he warned quietly, curious about sensed undercurrents and not too sorry that the attractive newcomer had apparently taken a dislike to the surgeon. With Tyler out of the running, he might have a chance to reach first base with the beautiful Venetia Keen!

'I dare say, but I fail to see how that can affect me, Howard. I'm good at my job, and that's all that matters, I imagine.' Venetia meant to be just as good at keeping the good-looking registrar at bay too, for she disliked his disturbing effect on her unsettled emotions. She had known the first day at Sandy's with all its associations wouldn't be easy, but she hadn't bargained for meeting someone like Tyler Petrie!

'Oh, sure. But you may not get too many opportunities to show off your skills if you alienate our Mr Petrie,' Howard pointed out drily. 'Linnie turns up for clinics and the occasional procedure, but he does a great deal of private work and he's got into the habit of leaving the major part of his Sandy's patients to Tyler. He's the real boss around here these days, you'll find.'

She shrugged. 'I'm not afraid of anything he can do,' she said scornfully, secure in Rogan's affection and her own excellent qualifications.

'Maybe not, but you'll be well advised to keep on the right side of the man. A wrong word here or there can hinder your progress on the career ladder, and I expect you're as ambitious as everyone else.'

Venetia *was* ambitious, but she had no intention of fluttering her eyelashes at Tyler Petrie to ensure future promotion at Sandy's, she told herself tartly, and adroitly changed the subject to the next procedure on that morning's list.

Later, accompanying the senior registrar on ward rounds, she forgot her resentment and her body's absurd reaction as they examined a number of patients together and discussed diagnoses and prognoses as professional people with a common aim, the welfare of those in their care.

Tyler was very good with the patients, putting them instantly at ease with a smile, just the right word, a reassuring pat of hand or shoulder and his obvious confidence as well as the impression that he had limitless time to listen to their fears and answer all their tentative questions. Men visibly relaxed as he allayed anxiety, and women promptly fell under the spell of his charm—and junior nurses almost fell over their own feet to attract his attention as they went about their ward routines. It was probably an excellent antidote to all that flattering interest that she remained cool, impersonal and totally unimpressed, Venetia decided drily.

She felt sufficiently confident to challenge him occasionally, disagreeing with a diagnosis or a suggested course of treatment, and his sensed approval pleased her because it centred on her ability rather than her femininity. Good looks and a shapely body were nature's gifts, after all. She'd had to work hard to earn a place on Rogan's firm, and it was satisfying that Tyler Petrie seemed to recognise and applaud her achievement.

She didn't like him any better for it, though. She had no respect for women-chasers, and the way he had kissed her, so masterful, so sure of her response, left her in no doubt of his sensuality or his casual attitude to her sex. She wasn't about to become one of his conquests. In any case, it was her vivacious sister that he really fancied.

She stayed late to write up essential notes on the patients who had become her responsibility. Tyler seemed in no hurry to leave either, apparently absorbed in *The Lancet*, but she refused to allow his presence to disturb her concentration. Finally finished, she shuffled her papers into neatness and stored them away in her briefcase.

Tyler glanced up from the medical journal as she got to her feet and exchanged her white coat for an unexpectedly dramatic jacket of bold, vibrantly colourful floral design, its beige background toning with the slim skirt and stylish shirt that had replaced her theatre greens earlier in the day. Her blonde hair swung about her face in a swirl of bright curls as she shook it free of her coat collar with a graceful shrug of narrow shoulders. She was beautiful, catching at his heart and stirring desire, melting the last, lingering trace of chagrin and wounded pride.

Throughout the day he had complied with her insistence on distancing the personal from the professional, but now he felt impatient with pretence, eager to sweep her from the aseptic hospital precincts to some private place where he could hold her in his arms and rediscover the girl who had so enchanted him at Trevor's party.

His smile was warm, caressing. 'Here endeth the first day. I hope we weren't too hard on you.' It had been a long, demanding day from that early start in Theatres to the final ward round after a seemingly endless afternoon in Outpatients. Tyler was tired, but Venetia looked remarkably fresh and very lovely, violet eyes in the grave, beautifully sculpted face regarding him with a hard to read expression in their shimmering depths.

'Not at all. I enjoyed it.' Venetia wondered why she lingered to talk when she only wanted to go home to her peaceful apartment and a light supper and an interesting book or TV programme. It wasn't wise to encourage him, she reminded herself sternly. 'It seemed like a holiday after the Marlborough, I assure you!'

Seventy-two hours on duty, snatching an hour or two of rest when and where she could, constantly stretched and always anxious that tiredness and a resultant lack of concentration might result in a fatal mistake, had been routine for a house surgeon at the busy general hospital in a run-down area of the city.

'It was an excellent training ground,' he remarked.

'It was certainly valuable experience. The stress of struggling to survive on a low income in a depressed neighbourhood is a contributory factor in cardiac disease, and I made it the subject of my thesis. But Sandy's is really the only place for an ambitious surgeon.'

'Yet you didn't apply for a job here when you left university?'

The warmth of his smile encouraged confidences, but Venetia hesitated to tell him too much. 'It didn't seem a good idea at the time,' she explained.

'Because your father was in charge of the CSU?'

'That was one of the reasons.' Another had been a reluctance to be lumped with her outrageous sister, a student nurse at Sandy's in those days, but she could scarcely say so, she thought drily.

Her apparent scruples didn't tally with his suspicion

that she hadn't hesitated to use her friendship with Rogan Linnie to her own ends. She was an enigma—but a very attractive one. 'Why not tell me the others over dinner?' On the confident words, Tyler rose, dwarfing the smaller, slighter girl with his impressive height and magnificent physique. 'We'll unwind over some food and a bottle or two of wine and get to know each other properly.'

Venetia backed from his overwhelming maleness. 'I've no desire to know you at all away from Sandy's,' she said firmly.

Tyler stifled a stir of impatience with a continuing charade. 'Come on, sweetheart, no more games,' he coaxed. 'We're both off duty and there's no one around, and I've been aching to kiss you again all day.' He reached for her, intent in his dark eyes, desire in the taut tension of his tall frame.

She took another step back. 'I advise you not to do so, however.' Ice dripped from the words.

As he laughed, soft and sensuous, she realised too late that the words had acted as a challenge. She turned to stalk from the room, affronted, but she was caught and held in a powerful and inescapable embrace. His strong arms enfolding her, his hard body pressed against her back, his breath warm on the nape of her neck as his sighing mouth swept her skin, she felt the tingling shock of his nearness lift the hair from her scalp and scamper all the way down her spine to her toes.

She gasped as he expertly swung her to face him and her breasts came into crushing contact with his massive chest. He smiled down at her with triumph in dancing dark eyes, and she realised with dismay that he was aware of her body's triggered reaction.

'You idiot! You're making another mistake. . .' she attempted furiously, but the words were lost in such a warm, sensually sure kiss that her mouth trembled in involuntary response to the seeking pressure.

'Am I?' He lifted his head to search her startled face for an instant before kissing her again.

A rippling tide of yearning took her by surprise. She couldn't believe what was happening to her, for she was a stranger to such sensations, such foolish, wanton weakness, such melting desire. Oh, she had been held and kissed and caressed in the past, and instinctively shrunk from a fever of passion that she unwittingly aroused and couldn't share and didn't quite know how to handle. Now, at last, she understood the longing and the need—and she was alarmed that a man she scarcely knew at all had the power to fill her with tremulous delight at a touch.

She broke free. 'If you ever do that again, you'll answer to a charge of sexual harassment before the Medical Council!' she stormed in sheer self-defence, shocked by the eager, treacherous flame he had ignited in the dark, secret centre of her body. Deep down, was she no different from Van with her succession of lovers, after all?

A dark eyebrow soared towards the crisp jet curls tumbling across the surgeon's brow. 'I don't believe this! You sound like the worst kind of feminist. Harassment, indeed! I don't understand you, Venetia.'

'Of course not! You don't know me!' she snapped.

Tyler sighed and shrugged. 'All right. Perhaps we *do* have a lot to learn about each other, but you don't seem a stranger when I'm holding you—and I swear that you feel the same about me,' he said softly, bewildered but willing to make allowances, to put up with any amount of feminine temperament, as long as he won her in the end.

Colour surged into already heightened cheeks. He was impossible, utterly insufferable! He just didn't listen to anything she said, too arrogantly sure of himself and his irresistible charm! 'I'm appalled by your colossal conceit,' she said coldly. 'Your caveman tactics might work with some women, but they don't appeal to me, Mr Petrie. Kindly keep your hands to yourself in future.' Seizing bag and briefcase, she stalked to the door.

Women were the very devil, Tyler thought wryly, half angry, half amused and very, very baffled. But he wasn't going to let this one walk away from him without making some effort to keep her. 'If you change your mind about dinner, I'll be in Perry's, waiting for you,' he called after her, referring to a nearby wine bar that was a favourite haunt of Sandy's staff.

Scorning to reply, Venetia stalked to the lift, too angry even to acknowledge friendly goodnights from the theatre staff. She stabbed at the call button, fighting for control, trembling with a mix of fury, frustration and unwilling attraction.

How dared he kiss her and stir up all those unwelcome feelings and undermine her status as a surgeon by treating her like a woman!

She fumed all the way down to the ground floor. But, at heart, she felt a tiny, foolish regret that she had rejected the invitation—and the man. For she might have finally convinced him that she *wasn't* Van and they could have begun again on a new and better footing. She didn't really dislike him so much, but it was infuriating that he persisted in mixing her up with a look-alike sister who wasn't like her at all in the ways that really mattered.

It was change-over time for the ward staff, and there was a flurry of uniformed nurses in Main Hall as Venetia emerged from the lift. One of them was her sister, walking with a white-coated doctor, looking very pretty and deceptively demure in her blue dress, blonde hair in a shining French plait beneath the crisp white cap of a staff nurse.

They were so startlingly alike that it wasn't surprising that a man who had met Van only briefly at a party should fail to distinguish one sister from the other on the following day, Venetia conceded fairly. Side by side, it was probably easy to tell them apart. At any other time, anyone might be forgiven for confusing them, although Van was the prettier, with huge violet eyes fringed with thick dark lashes and a smiling curve to her mouth that proclaimed her lighthearted attitude to life. Venetia had always been more seriously inclined than her sister, with her zest for life and her tendency to look upon nursing as a vehicle for meeting eligible men rather than a long-term career. Medicine, and surgery in particular, had been Venetia's whole life for some years, so it wasn't surprising that she was alarmed by the advent of someone like Tyler Petrie into her life.

Catching sight of her, Van hastily separated from her doctor friend and hurried to join Venetia by the heavy plate-glass exit doors. She was genuinely pleased to welcome her to Sandy's, although she deplored her sister's staidly uncompromising attitude to life—and men. In her view, both were meant to be enjoyed to the full.

'Just finished? Be an angel and give me a lift if you're going home?'

They lived separate, very different lives, and Van was currently sharing a terraced house in a nearby street with two friends, while Venetia had kept on the small but homely flat near the Marlborough, although it meant half an hour's drive each way in busy traffic. The two sisters crossed the staff car park to the bay where Venetia had left her gold-coloured Fiesta. Van didn't drive and claimed that she had no need to learn when there was no shortage of men willing to drive her wherever she wished to go.

Returning a curious glance from a young man who paused to stare at seemingly identical twins and sending him an encouraging smile, Van linked a hand in her sister's arm and said warmly, 'Tell me about your first day.'

'It went very well. Rogan was very kind, and the others made me very welcome. They're a friendly crowd.' One in particular had been more than friendly, Venetia thought drily, and hastily crushed the image conjured by her mind. She had no desire to dwell on a disturbing embrace when it was Van who should have been in those strong, demanding arms. Holding *her*, kissing *her*, paying *her* the doubtful compliment of his interest, had all been an absurd mistake.

'There's a man called Tyler. . . .' Unaware of the start of Venetia's heart at the throw-away words, Van swept on, 'I don't know if you came across him?'

'I expect you mean Tyler Petrie, Rogan's senior

registrar.' Venetia was surprised by the trace of uncertainty in her sister's tone, for Van usually contrived to know every detail about a new conquest within a very short time. 'I gather you met last night.' There was no point in pretending she didn't know about their encounter.

Van brightened. 'He told you? Then he's been talking about me!' She preened herself in obvious delight. Having waited all day for the surgeon to call her, ready to dismiss him just as airily if he'd lost interest overnight as some men did, she was pleased to learn that he hadn't forgotten all about her on parting with her in the early hours.

'Apparently he thought you worked in CSU,' Venetia explained.

'Idiot!' It was cheerfully indulgent. 'I *told* him Elizabeth Ward! He can't have been listening to a thing I said!'

'It seems to be a habit with him,' Venetia murmured drily.

But Van wasn't listening either. 'What did you think of him?' she demanded eagerly. 'He's a heart-stopper, isn't he?'

'I've been much too busy to notice.' Venetia unlocked the car doors.

Van slid into the passenger seat. 'You'll never go to heaven,' she mourned, mock-sorrowful.

The teasing dance of violet eyes compelled her sister to smile, to soften, to concede that perhaps she wasn't as immune as she pretended to the surgeon's physical charms.

'Oh, well, maybe I did notice,' Venetia conceded with a reluctant laugh.

'So I should hope! He's gorgeous! The most attractive man I've met in a very long time, anyway.'

'Sounds familiar,' said Venetia drily.

Van wrinkled her nose at the tone. 'Oh, I know you've heard it all before, but this time it's different. He really is something special,' she sighed.

'Aren't they all?' Gently mocking her sister's apparently incurable habit of falling headlong into love with a handsome face or a certain smile, Venetia ignored the tiny voice, deep down inside, that echoed the claim that Tyler Petrie was 'special', telling herself firmly that he was simply just another good-looking charmer with an abundance of sex appeal.

'So what was he saying about me? Do tell!' Van said eagerly.

Manoeuvring the car into the stream of slow-moving traffic on the busy main road that bordered the hospital grounds, Venetia thought wryly that this was one more time when she felt ten rather than just two years older than her impressionable sister.

'He was saying it about me, actually,' she said crisply. 'It must have been very dark or else he was very drunk when you met last night. I don't want to know any details, Van. I've a very good idea what went on between you. But he seems to think it was *me* he met at that party, and he's being rather heavy about it.'

Van's eyes widened in sudden mischief. 'You mean he's mixed us up?' It wasn't a surprise, for if she left her curling, shoulder-length hair to flow about her face as her sister usually did, few people could tell them apart. Her neat braid was ideal for the wards, but off duty she liked to let her hair down in more ways than one. 'Oh, what fun, Venetia! We could run him round in circles between us for weeks and he'd never be sure which of us he was dating!'

Venetia frowned. Trust her amoral, light-hearted sister to come up with such an outrageous idea, she thought crossly, carving up an unsuspecting motorist as the car shot across a crossroads, and hastily making amends with one of her loveliest smiles. 'I've no intention of playing that game or any other with a man like Tyler Petrie,' she declared firmly.

'You don't like him.' Van shot a shrewd glance at her sister's set face. 'I wonder why not.'

'He's a Casanova. I know the type.'

'Just *my* type.' It was a purr of almost feline satisfaction.

'Exactly.' Venetia suppressed a flicker of irritation that might almost be envy of her sister's casual attitude to amorous advances from good-looking surgeons.

'But what happened? Why are you so anti-Tyler? He seemed so nice. Did he make a pass or what?' The words were light, laughing, but inwardly Van was no more pleased or flattered than her sister that Tyler Petrie had confused their identities. For how *could* he have mistaken stuffy, cold-blooded Venetia for lively, fun-loving and warmly encouraging Van?

Realising that some of the day's events would probably filter through to Van via Sandy's very efficient grapevine, Venetia reluctantly provided a watered-down version of her encounters with the surgeon.

'I couldn't convince him that it wasn't me he met at that party,' she rounded off ruefully. 'He just wasn't listening. He thinks that I'm—*you*—are just playing hard to get, I'm sure. No doubt he expects me to turn up to meet him at Perry's in spite of all I said!'

'Why don't you?' Van was generously willing to forgo her own claim at this stage. She suspected that a persistently stubborn resistance to male attractions had been weakened by an encounter with a very sexy surgeon, and she wasn't convinced that Venetia was as indifferent as she pretended. It was about time that her sister realised there was more to life than her beloved surgery!

'Because I don't like him and I certainly don't trust him.' Knowing it would be more honest to admit that she didn't trust her own raging reactions to the man's sexuality, Venetia stopped the car outside Van's house and shook her head to an obviously dutiful invitation to stay for supper.

Later, about to slide her colourful jacket on a hanger and store it in her wardrobe, she paused, consumed by an absurd impulse to keep that date with the handsome registrar. The vision of him was so vivid that he might have been in the room with her—but no doubt it was prompted by the male scent of him that seemed to cling to her clothes and her skin.

Briefly she fantasised, remembering, recalling the warm mouth and the burn of his hands through the thin silk of her shirt, reliving the sear of desire as he crushed her close and the heavy thud of his heart against her breasts and the sudden, shocking but exciting awareness of his arousal.

Weakly, foolishly bereft of all rational thought for a few moments, she hungered for more of the paradise she had glimpsed in those strong arms, wanting him with all the urgency of newly-awakened emotions. Her body craved his closeness and his caress, and the liquid heat of longing urged her to sweep aside every other consideration but the desire for ecstatic fulfilment in his ardent embrace.

He was dangerous, Venetia realised on a gasp of alarm, reining the wanton thoughts and feelings. He was the only man she had ever known who could make her forget dreams, ambition and everything else with his slow, sweetly sensual kiss and the promise in his lean, powerful body.

He was a man to avoid.

CHAPTER THREE

BROAD shoulders hunched as he sat on a stool at the bar, nursing a beer, Tyler puzzled over the odd behaviour of a girl who blew hot and cold for no reason that he could define. He wondered if he could have said or done differently to bring about a more satisfactory end to the day than sitting by himself in Perry's with an absent woman on his mind.

He wanted the lovely Venetia Keen across a table from him, touching his hand, smiling into his eyes and encouraging him to carve a place for himself in her life. He wanted her in his arms, warm and soft and willing, easing the stresses and strains and vague disappointment of the day. He had never wanted any woman as he wanted her, and he wondered if it was the sensed intensity of his feelings that had caused her to back away. Or perhaps the intensity of her own desire?

Sensitive as well as sensual, Tyler knew that his touch, his kiss, his nearness had excited her, and surely that was only right and natural when he wanted her so much. Last night she had come close to surrender, he felt. Why then was she pretending now that nothing had happened between them?

Perhaps her involvement with Rogan Linnie was to blame for the overnight change of heart. Perhaps she was torn between the hope of advancing her career through the consultant's obvious interest in her and the way she felt about *him*.

35

Wishing he knew some at least of the answers, Tyler turned at a light touch on his arm.

'Hello, Tyler.'

Soft blonde curls tumbling about a lovely oval face, violet eyes smiling at him, pretty voice lilting his name with an encouragement that had been lacking all day—his heart somersaulted in surprised delight.

Heaven knew what game she was playing, but it didn't seem to matter when she gazed at him with limpid warmth in her beautiful eyes and her mouth shaped instinctively into a kiss that she leaned to bestow on him with such sweet self-assurance.

'I'd almost given you up.' He drew her into the curve of his arm and brushed his lips across the soft, scented hair, sighing his relief. 'What a chameleon you are!' It was a mix of amusement and exasperation.

'Am I?' Secrets danced in Van's eyes. She was very tempted to continue a charade that appealed so much to her impish sense of humour, but an intelligent man was unlikely to be fooled for long and might not forgive either the unwitting Venetia or herself.

Besides, there were a number of qualities in her clever, serious-minded sister that might appeal to someone like Tyler Petrie even more than her own happy-go-lucky self. So it might be wise to oust Venetia from his mind before it became irrevocably set on the wrong sister!

Tyler's dark eyes narrowed abruptly. Something felt wrong. It seemed too abrupt a change of attitude as she snuggled close, invitation in every line of her shapely body and sparkling in her smile. He hardly knew her, but somehow that struck him as out of character for the cool, unapproachable, businesslike girl he had observed from an enforced distance throughout the day. Her nearness warmed but didn't excite him, and that was puzzling too, for the earlier chemistry between them had been instantaneous and almost incandescent, a flame of passion that surpassed the stir of desire of the previous night.

Suddenly he noticed the mole at the corner of her mouth, small and dark, enticing a man's kiss. It might be merely cosmetic, stuck or painted on to enhance her appeal, but it didn't seem very likely, and the indignant protestations that had irked and challenged him abruptly took on a new meaning.

'You're not Venetia,' he said slowly.

Van twinkled up at him. 'I never pretended to be!'

He shook his head, incredulous. 'The likeness between you is extraordinary!'

'Then how did you know there are two of us?' Van was rather disappointed that the fun was over before it had really begun.

Tyler traced the smiling curve of her mouth with a long finger. 'You have a beauty spot. . .right here.' He paused. 'Venetia hasn't.'

So he'd made a detailed study of her sister's face! Van felt a stab of jealous pique, for he was even more attractive, more exciting, more of a man than she had recalled from a somewhat hazy encounter. Now, she had no more thought of tamely giving him up to Venetia than of flying to the moon—and she wondered just how hard her sister had tried to disillusion him as to her identity. For any woman, even one as indifferent to his remarkable good looks and fascinating charisma as Venetia claimed to be, would surely be tempted to make the most of such a golden opportunity!

'It's a give-away, isn't it? That mole?' She sighed. 'But not everyone notices it.'

'Then you've played this game before?' His mouth hardened as he suspected that the two girls had contrived to make him look foolish.

'It isn't a game, Tyler. I never said I was a surgeon,' Vanessa protested.

'You said you worked at Sandy's, and when I saw you this morning in theatre greens, scrubbing. . .' Tyler broke off, a wry expression in his dark eyes. 'Except that it wasn't you but your twin, of course.'

'We aren't twins—just sisters.'

'Whatever.' He lifted powerful shoulders in an impatient shrug. He scanned the lovely, laughing face, still shocked to learn that two Keen girls worked at Sandy's and wondering why he hadn't run into either of them before. 'It must lead to a lot of confusion, looking so alike.'

Van caught the note of disapproval in his deep voice and thought it unfair. They couldn't help looking like two peas in a pod, after all! 'It isn't usually a problem.' She didn't add that they had spent most of their adult lives working at different hospitals. 'We aren't really so alike. Venetia's the serious one, the dedicated doctor, the ambitious surgeon. Me—well, I just like to have fun.' She smiled up at him meaningfully, hugged his arm. 'She said you asked her to have dinner with you. Am I an acceptable substitute?' Laughter mingled with the warm flirtation in the dancing eyes.

'I thought I was asking *you*,' Tyler said drily.

'You were wasting your time asking my sister, that's for sure! She doesn't date.'

'Never?' He raised a sceptical eyebrow.

'Oh, she goes out with Rogan occasionally. They're very close. Rogan Linnie,' Van enlarged airily. 'Your boss, isn't he?' Blithely unaware that she had confirmed his suspicions about the couple, she swept on, 'Venetia hasn't a romantic bone in her body, I'm afraid. Men would probably interfere too much with her plans for the future. She's set her heart on a consultancy.'

Tyler had already realised that the new junior registrar was ambitious. Now, it seemed that even her sister knew that she would go to any lengths to achieve her ends. But, as he ordered drinks and steered the willing girl towards a table, he knew a deep-down determination to prevent the beautiful Venetia Keen from throwing herself away on the wrong man simply to secure a dream.

Tucking thick blonde hair into a mob cap as she came out of the changing-room, Venetia checked, her heart giving an odd little skip and a jump at sight of the tall surgeon. Tyler moved forward to intercept her, so handsome, such a dominant personality and somehow such a threat to her peace of mind. She looked up at him warily, trying not to recall the exciting, wayward dreams of this man that had disturbed her night's rest.

'I owe you an apology, Miss Keen,' he said formally, a wry smile crinkling the dark eyes. 'You were right and I was most embarrassingly wrong. You're *not* the girl I thought you were.'

She didn't smile. 'You've seen my sister.' It wasn't a question.

'Last night. She turned up to meet me in Perry's in your place.'

Venetia nodded. 'I thought she might.'

'Which is why you told her where to find me, no doubt,' he suggested drily.

'I expect so.'

Of course she had known that Van would rush to reclaim the man she probably regarded as her property on the strength of just one encounter. Her sister was very predictable. Having a very good idea how the evening had gone—and ended—Venetia sternly suppressed an instinctive pang of protest at the thought of them entwined in each other's arms. Van had seen him first, and there was no room in *her* life for a man like Tyler Petrie. One experience of that dangerous, distracting sexuality was quite enough for a girl who needed to keep her mind—and her heart—on the future she had planned for herself.

So, although it wasn't easy to ignore the devastating charm of his smile and the insistent tug at her emotions, she knew she must continue to keep him at a safe distance.

Looking into the lovely but remote face, Tyler ached to quicken those unsmiling lips to sweet response, longed to sweep her into his arms in spite of their clinical surroundings and the comings and goings of the theatre staff.

At the same time, irritation kindled at her cool, unrelenting attitude. Damn it, he had held her, kissed her, unmistakably fired her with the heat of his own fierce longing, and he resented being treated now as if he was still a stranger. . .and one that she didn't particularly like!

'Surely it would have been a simple matter to explain that you have a sister so like you that people have trouble telling you apart?' he queried.

Venetia shrugged. 'It didn't seem important,' she returned coldly, sensing accusation in the challenging tone and resenting the ease with which he contrived to put her in the wrong.

She had tried to explain. He just hadn't listened, so arrogantly sure that he was right, so stupidly stubborn that he was deaf to her protests, steamrollering her with his confidence and his kisses!

'Perhaps you hoped I'd look foolish when I eventually found out that I'd made a mistake? How disappointing for you that you missed the dénouement!' he drawled, on the edge of anger.

A theatre technician passed them, trundling a resuscitation trolley, glancing at them with casual curiosity that took in their tense, controlled figures. A nurse carrying a tray of instruments to the sterilising-room paused to stare at the tall, bristling surgeon in the well-cut grey suit and the slender, defensive newcomer in theatre greens, obviously sensing all the ingredients for a good gossip with her friends.

The bleep of Tyler's pager broke in on the angry moment, disturbing the comparative quiet of the corridor that belied the busyness of the theatre staff behind the scenes as they prepared the operating suites for the day's lists. The swing of an outer door coincided, heralding the arrival of Howard Wylie, and Venetia was abruptly reminded that she had yet to scrub.

'Shouldn't you answer that?' she said crisply, and brushed past the scowling registrar, cross with herself for caring as she saw the stormy outrage in the glinting dark eyes and the grim set to the sensual mouth.

She sympathised with him to some extent, she admitted, rinsing well-soaped hands and arms beneath the flow of running water. No man liked to look foolish, and it was easy to imagine the scene when Van had turned up at Perry's in her place, just as she had known that she would. They might be chalk and cheese in everything but looks, but she knew the way her sister's mind worked!

It was just as well that *she* had resisted the temptation to join him in the wine bar, for two look-alike dates would probably have turned the surgeon against both of them for ever! As it was, Van had no doubt enjoyed compensating him for his discomfiture.

It was absurd to regard her own sister as a rival for a man she really didn't want for herself, Venetia knew, but there was a tiny pocket of despondency in her mood as she joined the rest of the operating team in the theatre. For past experience had shown that most men preferred the lively, extrovert Van to herself— and why should Tyler be an exception just because he had kissed her in mistake for her sister?

Having learned his mistake, he had settled for Van. That was obvious from the formal apology, the flash of irritation and the slight coolness of his manner that she observed for the rest of the day.

However, there was too much to do and to learn in the new job to fret over a man she scarcely knew. It wasn't surprising if he was embarrassed and annoyed and had very little to say to her. After all, didn't her cheeks burn at the mere recollection of the way she had returned a stranger's ardent kisses?

Over the next few days, Rogan took her firmly under his wing and Venetia spent most of her time assisting him with procedures, trailing after him on ward rounds and sitting-in as he saw patients in the cardiac clinic.

His senior registrar had his own list and his own patients, and apart from the occasional conference, Venetia saw little of Tyler. Like most busy surgeons, he seemed to have too much on his mind to be more than distantly polite, and she took her cue from him, unaware that she disappointed him with her chilly, rebuffing attitude and her glowing response to everything that the consultant said and did.

It seemed to Tyler that ice-cold ambition set her beyond the reach of every man but the one with the power and the position to help further her career. She hung on Professor Linnie's every word and followed him around like a devoted disciple. He didn't know the full extent of the relationship between his boss and the new junior registrar, but it was probably a waste of time for him to go on wanting her, Tyler told himself impatiently—and knew he simply couldn't help himself.

It was more than an easily dismissed attraction. He was familiar with the sexual stir, the thrill of the chase, the challenge of possible conquest. This was different. He had known and accepted rebuffs from women in the past with a shrug of broad shoulders and a light heart, but the mere thought of losing Venetia to another man was shocking and disturbing, a threat to his entire happiness and peace of mind.

As Venetia made her way to the lift one evening, burdened with bag, briefcase and a number of books, Tyler fell into step at her side. 'Here, let me take those,' he said as the books threatened to slide from beneath her arm.

'Thank you.' She relinquished her load reluctantly. It would have been churlish to refuse the offer of assistance, but now she was committed to spending a few minutes in his company. She was seeing far too much of a man whose mere presence caused her heart to flutter wildly, but it seemed there was no escaping him.

The surgeon glanced at the titles of the medical tomes, heavy in both senses of the word. 'A little light reading, I see,' he murmured with a twinkle in his dark eyes.

Venetia stiffened at the intimately teasing tone. 'Essential studying for my Fellowship.'

He ushered her before him into the lift. 'I admire your dedication. But it will be some time before you're ready to take your Fellowship, surely? In the meantime, why not live a little? Dump the books and come for a drink.' He smiled at the slender girl in the oatmeal linen suit and soft cream blouse, admiring the glowing good looks and quiet elegance and the cool self-possession that he had once shattered with a kiss. 'You know what people say about all work and no play.'

'You'd find me a very dull Jill, in any case,' she told him firmly. 'If it's a playmate you want then I recommend my sister.'

'I like Van. She's a nice girl—no thorns.' Tyler scarcely knew what prompted him to praise one sister to the other, unless it was mild irritation with such determined defensiveness.

'Then I'm sure she'll be delighted to have a drink with you, Mr Petrie,' Venetia said sweetly.

'But I'm asking *you*, Miss Keen.'

She looked away from the warm persuasion in smiling dark eyes. 'I've a date with those books. Sorry.' She kept her gaze firmly fixed on the panel of rapidly changing lights as the lift carried them down to the ground floor. It was a spacious lift, designed for the conveyance of stretcher trolleys and porters and accompanying nurses, but she felt as if it was far too small for two people.

Tyler wasn't really a threat, however, keeping his distance with her books held against his broad chest, but her throat constricted and her heartbeat quickened in response to an unmistakable sexual tension—and all because she was alone with a good-looking charmer, she mocked the absurd tremor of apprehension.

As he followed her from the lift, she turned to him and held out her hand. 'I can manage now, thanks.'

Having no choice, Tyler handed over the books and watched her walk away, straight-backed, declaring her independent spirit with the set of her shoulders and the shining, held-high head.

He found it hard to cope with unaccustomed feelings of hurt and rejection. He had never felt quite so strongly about any woman, and he realised with a shocked awareness that he was in love for the first and possibly the last time in his life.

Getting nowhere with Venetia, he had continued to date Van now and again, but she was almost a carbon copy of all the other women he had known. First meeting had led to a swift, false enchantment that had been totally dispelled by greater acquaintance with the very different Venetia. Having briefly fancied one sister, he had plunged deep into love with the other. He had met his true destiny in the shape of a green-gowned girl with his own fierce dedication to surgery.

But it wasn't going to be easy to convince her that they were meant for each other. Ambition could be a very compelling master, and Tyler knew he had hurt several girlfriends in the past with his stubborn refusal to be distracted from the work that blatantly mattered more than they did. So maybe he deserved to be rebuffed now by a girl whose ambition was as acute as his own.

Arriving early the next morning, Venetia was gowned and gloved to assist with a heart valve replacement when Tyler strolled into the scrub annexe.

'Someone should have told you there was no need for you to scrub this morning,' he said by way of greeting. 'The professor won't be in today. He's in York—something to do with the new clinic that's his main interest these days.' Disapproval tinged his tone. 'I'm doing his list.'

It was blunt intimation that he didn't want her to assist him, and Venetia's heart sank. 'I thought you might be short of a surgeon on your team,' she ventured, wondering if he was punishing her for snubbing him last night and recalling Howard's warning that it was unwise to make an enemy of the senior registrar. 'I'll stay and watch, anyway. If you've no objection. . .?'

'Feel free.' Turning on taps, Tyler began to lather bare arms and strong hands. He had seen chagrin cross her lovely face, but even Rogan Linnie, emotionally involved with the girl, might think twice about letting her assist with life-threatening surgery on a critical newborn. There was really no need for him to feel reproached by the tilt of her chin and the accusation in violet eyes.

Studying his uncompromising back, sensitive to the wave of displeasure that emanated from his powerful frame, Venetia locked both arms across her breasts to stifle a vague hurt. 'About last night. . . I really did have work to do,' she said defensively.

'I'm sure you did.' He smiled at her over his shoulder. 'I took your advice, by the way. I had a drink with your sister.' By chance rather than design, in fact, running into Van and some of her friends when he dropped into Perry's for a drink before going home. But maybe it wouldn't do any harm to let Venetia think he had deliberately sought out her sister after she had said no to him.

'Oh. . .good. . .' Venetia walked from the room as a theatre nurse entered it with a fresh pile of sterile towels and spent the next ten minutes talking animatedly to Howard, whose uncomplicated friendliness massaged her deflated ego. She had held out an olive branch and had it brushed from her hand with that smiling allusion to her sister that left her in absolutely no doubt where she stood.

Later, banished to the rear of the theatre to watch as Tyler operated, taking care not to get in the way of busy nurses and having to crane her neck to see over the bowed backs of the surgeons, she felt she had been put firmly in her place as a newcomer.

She was no fool, and she realised that Rogan's kindly but blatant favouritism of recent days had done her no good at all in his senior registrar's critical eyes. Along with everything else, Tyler probably felt she was rather too big for her boots and had set about cutting her down to size. In more ways than one.

Venetia forgot the prickle of resentment as she followed the progress of those clever hands in the tiny cavity. It was the first time that she had seen him operate instead of assist, and she was impressed. Admiring the economy and the deceptive simplicity of his style, she stored up a number of useful tips for her own guidance. For one day, in the not too distant future, *she* would carry out such delicate and complex micro-surgery on an infant with a similar confidence, knowing that a new life was dependent on her skills for its survival, determined to do her best for small patient and anxious parents as well as the reputation of the Cardiac Unit that her own father had established at Sandy's.

She did her best to concentrate on the procedure, but, watching Tyler, she was alarmed by a persistent tendency to recall the earlier enchantment in those smiling eyes and the magic in a kiss. Tall and darkly handsome, popular with staff, colleagues and patients for much more than his charismatic charm, clever and caring and genuinely interested in people and their problems, he was a thoroughly nice person—and much too attractive for comfort, threatening more than her peace of mind.

However, she was unlikely to lose anything more than her foolish heart to a man who had obviously lost all meaningful interest in her once he found Van again.

CHAPTER FOUR

TYLER was totally absorbed, his mind and hands working in skilled unison, needing all his concentration for his task. He snapped at a nurse who dropped a metal receiver at a vital moment and growled at the assisting surgeon who was fractionally slow to obey an urgent instruction.

But he was quick to make amends for the small spurts of irritation with a smiling glance for the offending nurse and a quiet word of praise for Keith Golding when the anxious moment had passed, Venetia noticed.

She found herself warming to him a little more each day. She didn't want to like him, to feel that he was a man that any woman would want to love, but he seemed to have a fatal attraction for her, she thought wryly.

'He reminds me very much of your father,' Ray Owen murmured in her ear. One-time house surgeon and one of Van's former loves, he had wandered in to watch proceedings during a break in his own operating list.

Venetia stared. 'There isn't the slightest resemblance!' she protested.

'Oh, not in looks,' he agreed instantly. 'The Old Man was leonine, with that flowing blond hair and massive build. Tyler's more the panther type,' he grinned.

More interested in what was going on with the patient than in Ray's superfluous remarks, Venetia didn't answer. But, studying the surgeon with his dark hair and bronzed good looks and lean, lithe build, she admitted his grace, the ripple of smooth muscle, the element of stealth and surprise and the promise of power that justified the lighthearted reference to a panther.

'There's something about him. . .*presence*, I suppose. He has much of your father's style and even some of his mannerisms. Look at the way he holds his head and that glance round the team before and after each major step. Just like the Old Man. I could never make up my mind if he was simply checking that we were all still awake or expecting a round of applause!'

Venetia smiled dutifully and shifted position for a better view, wishing he would shut up and let her concentrate on a particularly tricky part of the proceedings.

'A man with a brilliant future, I'd say,' Ray swept on, apparently unable to take a hint. 'Totally dedicated and single-minded about his work. Great hands, too. I suppose you know he's just back from Australia? He went on a courtesy visit to a Perth hospital and carried out a heart-lung transplant for a cystic fibrosis sufferer that went down so well that he was offered a consultancy. . .'

She nudged the garrulous surgeon into silence as Tyler shot a scowling glance in their direction, no doubt distracted by the sibilant whispering. A few moments later, Ray was called away by the arrival of his own patient and Venetia was free to return her attention to the drama of open-heart surgery taking place in the theatre.

Observing Tyler in the light of Ray's casual comments, she had a sudden vision of her father with just that tilt to his big, blond head, just that glow in his eyes as he worked at the shaping and sculpting of clay that had been his main relaxation after a day in Theatre. Having been banned from watching him work with the assurance that she had an excellent teacher in his most respected rival, Professor Hutton of the Marlborough's CSU, and would only pick up some of *his* bad habits, Venetia had no way of comparing surgical styles, but she knew he must have looked just like Tyler in tense moments in the operating theatre.

It was that air of devotion to his work and that supreme confidence in his skilled hands that stamped the senior registrar with a likeness to a man who had known so many surgical triumphs during his time at Sandy's, she decided. She might resent his arrogance and his compelling sensuality, but she applauded the caring concern that was conveyed through those strong, sure hands.

Venetia felt that he willed the survival of his tiny patient with the sheer force of a very powerful personality. He seemed to be a man who knew just what he wanted—and how to make it happen.

He worked in near-silence for much of the time. She compared the quiet tension of the operating theatre with the light-hearted asides, the mild flirtations and the animated discussion of cricket scores and Wimbledon results and golf handicaps that seemed to accompany Rogan's procedures. As a highly respected consultant at the top of his particular tree, Rogan could afford to be more relaxed about his work, she supposed. His senior registrar was still in the process of proving that he was just as able as his boss—and *she* had a very long way to go before she could hope to match either of them for skill or experience.

She could probably learn a lot from Tyler. So, instead of clashing with him at every turn, perhaps she ought to be paving the way to a better relationship with a practical eye to her future at Sandy's.

Rogan was often away, lecturing, operating at other hospitals and private clinics, attending medical conferences. At such times, Tyler took over his patients and the operating lists. It was obvious that he could make or break a junior colleague's career if he chose—and he had already exercised a little of that power that morning, Venetia realised. She might often find herself on the perimeter of theatre activity, as now, watching and fretting instead of honing her own surgical skills as a useful member of the team.

It was a risk that she would simply have to take, however. For even ambition couldn't persuade her that it would be wise to encourage a man who triggered alarm bells at a touch.

It was a lengthy procedure, made even longer by constant crises as the delicate heart threatened to fail or the weakened lungs came close to collapse. At such times, only prompt action by surgeons, anaesthetist and theatre nurses prevented disaster. An audible sigh of relief rippled through the operating-room when the last suture was successfully tied.

'How is she, Howard?' Working against difficult odds on a critically ill baby, Tyler had done all he could to ensure a future for her, but he wasn't too optimistic about the outcome.

'She's as stable as we've any right to expect, in the circumstances,' the anaesthetist temporised, checking the tubes and wiring that linked the baby girl to a ventilator and adjusting the flow of a drip to his satisfaction. 'The next few days are going to be critical, of course.'

Tyler agreed. 'She really needs nursing on a one-to-one basis, but that's difficult with the present staff situation. I'll have to see if I can use my influence with Sister SCU.'

'Lila Murray's on duty today. Didn't you ditch her a couple of months ago?' Howard said slyly. 'Sweet talking isn't likely to get you anywhere with her, is it?' He nodded to the ODA and the nurse who waited to transfer the patient to the Special Care Unit and accompanied them to ensure that all was well during the short journey.

The rest of the team drifted from the theatre to relax until it was time for the next procedure or ward round or clinic. Theatre nurses began to clear away drapes and used instruments and clean the operating-room, and Venetia lingered to chat to one of them, a friend of Van's, her gaze on the surgeon who had moved away from the table, drawing down his mask.

Brow beaded with sweat, broad shoulders slumped, the strain of long, tense concentration shadowed the lean, handsome face. There was an air of despondency about his tall frame as he tugged at the strings of his gown, and she had to suppress a foolish urge to go to him and put her arms about the tired surgeon.

He didn't need her sympathy, her support, however.

There were plenty of women only too willing to open their arms to the good-looking Tyler Petrie. Van for one, so soft and feminine and alluring that no one could blame him if he had abruptly lost all interest in her prickly sister—and it would be a very good thing if he had, common sense insisted loudly to silence the odd little pang of protest in Venetia's breast.

Having acquired her defensive thorns during the years of study and hard work at the Marlborough that had gained her the present job at Sandy's, she would probably find them very useful in keeping Tyler at bay if he did persist in his pursuit of her. Van could allow her heart to rule her head, and frequently did, but she had no ambition beyond marriage. It was very different for herself. Her career was much more important than a vague yearning for an attractive senior registrar— and *her* heart was set on a brilliant future.

Wondering why she had to keep reminding herself of that fact since the first embarrassing encounter with Tyler, Venetia followed him into the annexe. Still feeling slightly disgruntled that she had been merely a spectator instead of taking part in the proceedings, she didn't smile at the man who was in the act of bundling his stained gown into a bin. She began to discard her own still pristine theatre gown without speaking.

'Things went very well on the whole,' he said easily. 'I think she'll do. . .' He used the traditional term that confidently forecast a good recovery from surgery or serious illness. 'I don't know if you could see all that was going on from your position, Venetia?'

'Pretty well, thanks.'

The cool tone and the lack of an answering warmth in her beautiful eyes told Tyler that she wasn't prepared to yield an inch to meet him halfway. Yet even at the very peak of concentrated effort, he had sensed the strangely supportive intensity of her watching gaze and felt she was with him every step of the way. He wished he could be as sure of her interest and attention outside the operating theatre.

'It won't be long before you're doing that one and *I'm* watching you,' he said with a smile that was meant to console her obvious disappointment at being excluded from the team that morning.

Venetia shrugged. 'I'd like to think so, but I'm beginning to learn that there are more obstacles than ordinary competition in the way of getting where I want to go,' she said drily, sure he would block her progress at Sandy's when and where he could if she continued to keep him at arm's length.

There was no doubt in her mind that he could and would smooth her path if she was nicer to him, but she had no intention of furthering her career via the clinical couch. She would make it to the top with or without Tyler Petrie's help!

Tyler arced an eyebrow. 'Feeling hard done by?' The understanding in his dark eyes caressed the stony face and taut figure of the aggrieved girl. 'I know you were hoping to assist, but we ran the risk of losing Holly at any time, as you saw.' He smiled at her. 'I didn't want that experience for you in your first weeks with the CSU.'

'It's nice of you to be so concerned,' she said drily. 'But I had to deal with all kinds of emergencies in my time at the Marlborough, usually because there were never enough senior staff around in a crisis. I'd have coped.'

'I was thinking of the inevitable inquiry if things had gone badly wrong.' As she was the newest and most junior member of the firm, her ability and her amount of theatre experience might have been called into question if the patient had died during surgery. He had been genuinely concerned that Venetia shouldn't start her career at Sandy's under a slight cloud. But she seemed to be suspicious of everything he said or did.

Venetia looked away from the glow of his gaze, fighting the unnerving tug of attraction. 'You don't have to explain anything to me, Mr Petrie,' she assured him crisply, taking refuge in the gulf between their professional standing. 'You're the boss. You make the decisions. I'm just here to do as I'm told.'

Tyler frowned at the chill formality. 'Then you won't mind taking charge of the patient for the next few days,' he said with a similar briskness. He could be just as formal if that was the way she wanted it, although he hoped she would eventually thaw and give him a chance to make amends for the bad beginning that had led to the present strain in their relationship. 'I'd like you to do the two-hourly observations and let me have regular reports.'

'Through the night too?'

'You've no objection, I hope? That's the critical period, obviously, and I don't want to lose her at this stage. The SCU staff are rushed off their feet, and I need someone with your intuition and your experienced eye to check her frequently and spot any danger signals if and when they arise.'

'I'll do my best,' she told him. The tight tone rejected the smooth-as-silk compliment that did nothing to alleviate her instinctive dismay at the assignment.

'Don't delegate the job, will you? She's *your* baby.'

His smile came and went so quickly that it ought not to have quickened her pulses with its fleeting enchantment. 'Very well,' she agreed.

'Let me know immediately if there's the slightest change in her condition. I'll give you a number where you can reach me when I'm off duty. . .' Tyler turned away, disheartened by the hardness of the violet eyes and the frosty set to the lovely mouth.

He wondered if he'd ever overcome the dislike and the prejudice of a girl who promised to matter more than anything else in the world to him, even his work. Just now, it seemed unlikely that he would ever hold her again, but the stir of his blood told him that Venetia belonged in his arms and in his heart.

Possibly for ever. . .

Alarmed by an instinctive response to his insidious charm, Venetia whipped up resentment and glowered at the surgeon's broad back as he strolled from the annexe.

It was the Marlborough all over again! Except then it had been compulsory for her to be on call through the night on occasions, and now it seemed that she had a choice. Except that it was *no* choice, the way he'd said it, making it impossible for her to refuse, she thought crossly.

House surgeons expected to be on duty at all hours of the day and night. It was part of the job. But registrars, even very junior ones like herself, felt that they had earned the right to regular hours as well as the authority to delegate certain jobs to even more junior colleagues. Tyler seemed to be indifferent to the fact that all her plans for the evening had been turned upside down by his arrogant dictate too.

As it happened, she'd only meant to do some essential studying, but he didn't know that, and she bristled with indignation. Maybe there *wasn't* anyone that she might want to put before the needs of a patient, but he didn't know that either! It rankled that he assumed her social life to be so non-existent that he had no need to apologise for disrupting it or to ask if it would be convenient for her to stay on call.

It would obviously be impractical to drive back and forth between hospital and home at two-hourly intervals throughout the night, so she would have to stay at Sandy's—and do the next day's work on whatever sleep she managed to snatch. Shades of the Marlborough, indeed!

Venetia knew it would be useless to make a protest, however. For all his charm, the velvet of that sense-stirring voice, Tyler Petrie was a man of steel.

Stalking in Tyler's wake on her way to the changing-rooms, she turned as someone called her name to see Howard Wylie hurrying along the corridor. She paused and waited for him to reach her, smiling.

He was slightly breathless from the hasty ascent of several flights of stairs from the Special Care Unit, two floors below. The lifts were very busy at that time of the day and he had been particularly anxious for a private word with Venetia before she left Theatre.

'Do you like opera?' he demanded with almost boyish eagerness. 'I've managed to get tickets for Pavarotti at the Garden. First night, too! I hope you'll come with me, if you're not doing anything this evening?'

'Oh, Howard! I'd have loved to go with you, but I can't,' Venetia said regretfully. She *did* like opera, but it didn't seem possible to seek out Tyler and explain and tell him she couldn't observe Holly that night, after all. 'I have to work tonight. Tyler's asked me to do the observations on Holly, and that means I can't leave the hospital.'

Howard frowned. 'He had no right to do that. Latimer's the house surgeon.'

It *was* Paul Latimer's job to look after the critical post-ops, of course. Venetia wondered why it hadn't occurred to her to point that out to Tyler. Surely she was long past the stage of feeling flattered because a senior surgeon entrusted a particular patient to her care?

'Yes, I realise that. But he's so busy. Tyler's very concerned that someone should keep a special eye on Holly for a few days,' she placated the obviously disappointed anaesthetist. 'I couldn't refuse.'

'There are more than enough SCU nurses to keep a special eye on one small baby, I'd have thought,' he persisted.

'Apparently not. I *can't* say I won't do it— not even for Pavarotti! Not now!'

She could, of course. Tyler wouldn't hesitate to release her from responsibility for Holly if she explained, she knew. But Venetia felt diffident about approaching him and oddly more reluctant to let him down than to disappoint the friendly, likeable Howard. She wondered why it was so important to be in the senior registrar's good books when she was doing all she could to discourage him from liking her at all.

'Tyler's taken it for granted that you will, I suppose.

He can be very autocratic,' Howard warned her disapprovingly. 'You shouldn't allow him to get away with piling extra work on you, Venetia.'

'Oh, I won't in future,' she assured him hastily, and sped away to change from theatre greens into a tan linen skirt and paisley silk shirt and don her white coat for ward rounds.

She kept a careful eye on the time and went along to the SCU for the first check on Holly and to get acquainted with the specially trained nurses who would be taking care of the sick baby, along with all the others in the Unit.

Two-day-old Holly was small and still and deceptively rosy from the anaesthetic, the erratic bleep of the monitor and the amount of equipment that surrounded her tiny frame in the incubator betraying that there was particular cause for concern about her condition.

Venetia had already met the anxious parents. The mother was getting over an emergency Caesarean and had been put in a side ward of the SCU to be near her critically ill baby. Mr Adams went off to the cafeteria for a meal, and Venetia drew a chair to the side of his wife's bed to listen and sympathise as she talked of the years of trying for a child, the joy when a fertility drug had resulted in the longed-for pregnancy and the shock of learning that the much-wanted little girl had a serious heart defect.

'Is she going to be all right, Doctor?' Mrs Adams asked anxiously. 'The nurses don't say very much to me, you know. I'm ever so worried. . .'

Venetia felt it would be wise to warn her that Holly was still very ill in spite of remedial surgery. Tyler had done everything he could, but sometimes a miracle was needed to save the life of a premature, possibly brain-damaged and dangerously ill baby. Holly was clinging to life at the moment, but the situation could change drastically, and she was well aware that she might have the dreaded and difficult task of telling the hopeful parents that all the efforts of surgeons and nurses had been in vain.

'Mr Petrie is a marvellous surgeon, one of the very best in cardiac surgery, and no one could have done more for Holly. All our nurses are trained to take special care of babies like Holly too. I know you and your husband are desperately worried about her and I'm not going to pretend that there's no cause for anxiety. But your little girl is a fighter, and that's half the battle, believe me,' she said warmly.

'Everyone's so kind. . .' Cheryl Adams swallowed bravely. 'No one could have been nicer to us than you and the nurses. We're ever so grateful. . .'

Venetia smiled and patted the woman's hand. 'Just doing our job.'

'But it isn't just a job to people like you and Dr Petrie, is it? You're dedicated, aren't you?'

'I suppose we must be,' she agreed lightly, and got an odd glow of satisfaction from the linking of their names in that touching accolade.

As she came and went throughout the day, at regular intervals, making the routine checks and entering her findings on Holly's chart, Venetia wondered a little drily why she had been assigned to look after his small patient when Tyler seemed to be in and out of the Special Care Unit almost as often as herself, running the rule over the baby and taking time to reassure Mr and Mrs Adams but apparently too rushed for more than a brief word with herself.

That was just how it should be, of course. There was really no need for him to linger, to chat, to start tongues wagging as they inevitably would if the much-admired surgeon seemed to pay her more than a professional attention. Throughout the day, they were both too busy for personal exchanges, in any case. Later, officially off duty like herself, Tyler no doubt had someone waiting for him when he looked in to check on Holly and left again within minutes.

The unit nurses fluttered around him and discussed him avidly after he had left, and some of their comments on the surgeon's busy love-life inevitably reached her ears as Venetia lingered to watch the monitor that registered Holly's heartbeats or to adjust the flow of a drip. She knew that much of the gossip must be wildly exaggerated, but even so it seemed that Tyler had a reputation for light loving and short-lived affairs.

All the more reason for keeping a firm grip on feelings that threatened to run away with her simply because she couldn't forget the magic in a kiss.

CHAPTER FIVE

TIME seemed to hang rather heavily on Venetia's hands
between visits to the SCU. The tempo of the day had
slowed down and there were fewer nurses on duty,
fewer people about in the corridors. She wrote some
letters, read *The Lancet* from cover to cover, studied
some case histories in readiness for ward rounds on the
following day and began to feel badly in need of a
break from all things relating to her job.

She felt very tempted to cross the road to spend an
hour in Perry's, so popular with Sandy's staff that it
was almost an extension of the hospital, regarded as
meeting place and social club, although little actual
drinking seemed to be done within its walls. She was
sure to find someone she knew in the wine bar that
evening. But on his last visit to the SCU, Tyler had left
the telephone number of Perry's and the message that
he would be there for most of the evening if he was
needed. Venetia didn't want him to suppose she was
following him, angling to spend some time with him.

Going along to check on Holly at ten o'clock, she
found the senior registrar there before her, stethoscope
resting gently on the small, shallow-breathing chest.
He seemed to be unaware of her as she approached,
and Venetia had a moment or two to observe the
tenderness in his touch, the concern in his deep-set
dark eyes.

Warming to him, she wondered why she fought so

hard against liking the caring, conscientious surgeon. Then he turned his darkly handsome head to look at her as she reached him, and the linger of love for his tiny patient in those expressive eyes shook her heart and she realised that she had lost the battle some time since. Working with him, getting to know him better with each day, it was proving impossible not to like him.

'How is she?' she asked briskly, crisply professional to conceal the flood of dangerous sentiment.

'Holding her own. . .just.' Straightening, Tyler slipped the stethoscope into the deep pocket of his white coat. 'She's a pretty little thing, isn't she?' he said softly.

Venetia looked at the crumpled pink bud of a mouth and the button nose, the delicate brows and the puzzled gaze of dark blue eyes dominating a doll-like face, the crown of soft black hair clinging damply to the tiny head, and felt a stir of the maternal instinct that was in danger of being crushed out of existence by her insistence on following a dream. Ambition left no room for thoughts of marriage and motherhood. But a child of his would look like Holly, a cluster of black curls and glinting dark eyes and a heart-catching beauty, she thought inconsequentially.

'You like children, don't you?' she said. It was an impulsive, slightly shy introduction of a personal note into very clinical surroundings.

'I like people,' Tyler amended with a flash of his beguiling smile. 'Isn't that what brought you and me into the caring profession in the first place—liking people, wanting to do what we could to help them?

Unless you had a different motivation? Like pleasing your father, for instance?'

'It did please him, but I don't think that's what prompted me to choose surgery.' Venetia frowned, for she had never bothered to analyse the long-cherished dream, simply accepted its urgings and worked hard to make it come true. 'I suppose it may have had something to do with pleasing Rogan. . .' she added, recalling an impressionable teenager's crush and Rogan's tactful handling of it. A lesser man might have bruised her shy sensitivity or taken advantage of her innocence or destroyed the frail bud of her self-esteem. He had been kind, understanding, and she had soon outgrown the youthful folly of thinking she loved him.

Dark brows shot together at the revealing admission. 'Then you and Linnie go back a long way?'

'Oh, we've known each other for years,' Venetia agreed, her tone warmer than she knew. 'I've always admired him tremendously, and perhaps he influenced my choice of career to some extent. He's certainly encouraged me all the way, and I'm really thrilled to have the chance of working with him.'

'You'll be working with *me* most of the time,' Tyler told her bluntly, brusque with jealous dislike of a long and possibly intimate association. 'You must have gathered that we don't see much of the professor in the unit these days. He does a great deal of private work and he's devoting a lot of his attention at the moment to the new clinic he's helping to establish in York. I believe he means to give up his consultancy here at Sandy's to devote all his time to it, in fact.'

'Really? He hasn't said anything about that to me.' Venetia glanced at the registrar's darkly brooding face, surprised by the harsh note in the deep voice. 'Is that an opportunity for you?' she asked, a little uncertainly, wondering if he would resent the intrusion on his private hopes and plans.

He shrugged. 'Maybe. I'm not sure that I'm interested. I've been offered a very similar consultancy in Perth and I may decide to accept.' It had never been a serious consideration until that moment, but if he was tumbling into love with a girl who had set her heart on Linnie, then there was little point in staying around to be tortured by watching the affair progress to its inevitable conclusion.

Putting half the world between them might be the only sensible thing to do.

Venetia bent her head over Holly's chart to hide a rush of dismay, such a foolish and totally needless reaction when it couldn't matter in the slightest if a man she scarcely knew went to the other side of the world and she never saw him again.

In fact, she almost wished he *would*! For then she might be able to concentrate on her job instead of dwelling on the thought of his sensual mouth and strong hands and lean, hard body with its power and its promise of thrilling, throbbing excitement and ecstasy.

A fall of shining blonde hair swung across her face as she lowered her head to enter figures on the chart in her neat script. Tyler conquered the urge to brush it away, to stroke the soft, slightly flushed cheek with a loving hand, to clasp the slim shoulder and turn her towards him for an exchange of kisses.

The SCU was no place for such feelings, but he burned with a fever of longing and it was torment to have her so near, to be so aware of her warm, sweet femininity and the delicate perfume of her hair and skin, and yet be barred from the trembling delight of holding her. At the back of his mind lingered the memory of a brief yielding, the involuntary arching and the thrust of taut, rounded breasts as a shiver of arousal rippled through the slender girl he held in his arms. It was impossible to believe that she was as indifferent to him as she pretended. The chemistry between them was so potent and so powerful that she must melt in the flame that would surely leap if lips and bodies came together again in that incandescent fusion.

She haunted him day and night with the pale cameo of her lovely face, the indescribable sweetness of her mouth and the inscrutable gravity of those violet eyes. Tyler was consumed with a determined desire, but he wanted so much more than the stir of sexual attraction, the tumult of sexual contact and the tempestuous peaks of sexual satisfaction. He wanted the caring and the sharing and the total commitment of a loving that involved hearts and minds as well as the mutual pleasuring of bodies.

For the first time in his thirty-four years, he wanted marriage. . .

Holding the thermometer to the light to check the reading, Venetia could scarcely concentrate on the silver thread of mercury that had crept a little higher on the glass tube. In spite of her anxiety over the sick baby, she was swept with such a tide of longing that it was almost as if the surgeon had touched her with a tender hand. Her body tingled from head to toe with an electric shock of desire that startled her unsuspecting heart as much as her senses.

Dear heaven, was she falling in love with this man?

Backing instinctively from such an alarming thought, she sped into protective speech. 'Temperature's up another degree. Cause for concern, do you think?'

He frowned. 'There's nothing really concrete to go on apart from the slight rise in temperature, but I've a gut feeling that things aren't quite as they should be,' he said thoughtfully. 'If it becomes necessary to rush her back to the theatre then I shall need you to assist, Venetia. So don't go home tonight, will you? I think we should both get some sleep while we can. I'll be just along the corridor in the duty surgeon's room if you need me.'

He walked away, more abruptly than he had intended, feeling it was imperative to put space between them before he forgot their clinical surroundings, the interested nurses, the sick infant and everything but the painful need to hold her in his arms.

Venetia felt a little consoled for the virtually sleepless night ahead of her by the thought that Tyler would be close at hand. It seemed he had no plans to go home either—wherever that might be. She knew so little about the surgeon—background, family, personal affairs—that it was particularly absurd to feel he had the power to change the entire course of her life, she scolded herself.

Hospital by night was a very different place from hospital by day, Venetia mused as she descended echoing stone stairways and walked through a number of deserted departments on her way to the cafeteria, shortly after midnight. She hadn't taken Tyler's advice to get some sleep, remaining in the SCU to talk to the night staff and help where she could and monitor Holly's temperature, so she had been on hand to cope with a minor crisis of a blocked drip without disturbing the presumably sleeping surgeon.

The dimly lit wards on the upper floors were hushed as patients slept or stirred and nurses went about familiar routines as quietly as they could, always alert for an anxious call or sudden, urgent summons.

Outpatients was a ghost town of silent corridors and empty consulting-rooms and shuttered reception areas, and only a night porter was around to nod to Venetia from his station at the big desk in Main Hall as she passed through it in her white coat and sensible shoes.

The Accident and Emergency Department never closed, however. Day and night, ambulances arrived at frequent intervals to discharge their cargo of sick, injured or despairing. Assisted by an able team of nurses, overworked casualty officers coped with a succession of shocked, disorientated patients as well as anxious and sometimes hysterical relatives and friends, dealt with a number of crises, tended minor or serious injuries and gave advice in between arranging for X-rays and blood tests, calling on specialist staff, ringing round the wards to find a bed for an urgent admission or alerting Theatres for emergency surgery.

Like all doctors in training, Venetia had done her stint in Casualty, and still wondered how she had survived the experience!

Before she returned to the SCU, she called into A & E to talk to an old friend from medical student days at the Marlborough who had transferred to Sandy's to be near her boyfriend.

Diane was busy but delighted to see her. 'How are you settling down in the new job?' she asked in a brief lull between diagnosing a case of acute appendicitis and stitching an earlobe that had been badly torn by a brutal tug at a young man's ear-ring during a drunken brawl.

'I feel as if I've been here all my life.' Venetia stifled a yawn and laughed, a little wryly.

'Long day?' It was sympathetic. Diane knew all about long days and even longer nights.

'Not as long as yours, I imagine. At least I'm officially off duty at the moment. I'm just keeping an eye on a critical post-op who may have to go back to theatre if she doesn't improve.'

'I'm glad I decided against becoming a surgeon. This is about as much responsibility as I can handle—and I was never much good at needlework,' Diane added with a grin.

Venetia laughed. 'Sewing up is the easy part!'

'I'll leave it to the experts like you.' Diane swung off on another tack. 'Van must be delighted that you've joined the staff. You haven't seen much of each other in the last few years, have you? I know you aren't exactly close, but you *are* sisters.' She was an only child herself, and her words were wistful. 'By the way, I hear she has a new conquest—one of the CSU surgeons. Rumour has it that he was all over her at a party the other night.'

'I'm not up to date on her love-life,' shrugged Venetia. No need to ask which surgeon was said to be Van's latest love—and if the grapevine was already busy with rumours then it must be a serious affair. Well, it ought to be a relief to know she had no need to worry about keeping the dangerously attractive Tyler Petrie at bay, after all. Like most men, he had soon discovered that one sister was nothing like the other except in looks—and which one to pursue for a fun time without strings.

'How about your own? Or is it still almost non-existent?' Diane teased gently. Studying her friend's lovely, guarded face, she wondered if Venetia could really be as content as she seemed with the evenings that were mostly spent with her books. 'You don't know what you're missing!' With a complacent smile, she pointedly admired the brand-new engagement ring on her own left hand.

'Yes, I do. Van tells me constantly,' Venetia said drily. She smiled warmly at her friend. 'I'm thrilled for you and Mike, of course, but I'm really not interested in that kind of involvement for myself. Not for a few years, anyway.'

'I'm not suggesting anything heavy. Just an occasional night out and some fun with an attractive bloke—there are lots to choose from here at Sandy's. How about Howard Wylie? You know him, don't you? He's very nice and he doesn't have a girlfriend at the moment. You could do worse. Why don't we make a foursome one evening?'

'Don't matchmake for me, Diane! Howard *is* nice and we get on quite well, but he isn't really my type.' Until she had arrived to take up her new appointment at Sandy's, Venetia hadn't honestly known which kind of man was her type—but it appeared to be the tall, dark and much too good-looking kind who could apparently take his pick from a dozen girls. 'In any case, it will take me all my time to justify my place with the CSU, keep up with all the new developments in cardiac surgery and study for my Fellowship,' she went on firmly. 'I can't see how love could possibly fit into that schedule.'

'Love doesn't wait to be fitted in,' Diane warned shrewdly. 'It just hits you—*pow!*'

'Remind me to dodge.' Venetia got to her feet as a nurse put her capped head round the door to advise the Casualty Officer that the victims of a traffic accident were en route to A & E. 'Come for a meal one evening—you and Mike,' she invited warmly, strolling along the corridor by her friend's side. 'I'd like to meet him at long last, and we can really catch up on each other's news.'

'Love to. . .' Diane was gone on a flurry of white coat and dancing chestnut curls as the sound of an approaching ambulance siren caused a bustle of urgency among her colleagues in the A & E.

Venetia made her way back to the SCU, trying not to be tormented by the image of Tyler and Van in each other's arms that had been created in her mind by Diane's light remarks. After all, she had known from the beginning that it was Van he really wanted. The wave of interest and admiration that had seemed to swamp her only a couple of hours ago could only have been a flight of fancy on her part. Or the briefest stir of desire in a very physical man, not to be taken seriously by any sensible woman.

After the two o'clock observations, she retired to the small room that had been allocated to her for the night by Sister, confident that the SCU nurses would alert her if necessary. She showered and slept, then scrambled hastily into her clothes once more at the four o'clock summons from the switchboard.

Thankfully, she registered the lowering of the temperature that indicated a slight improvement in Holly's condition. Tyler had asked to be informed of the slightest change, so she felt no compunction about disturbing the sleeping surgeon.

Listening to the burr-burr on the other end of the line, Venetia lifted the weight of thick blonde hair from the nape of her aching neck, fighting a rush of weariness. It was easy to lose the habit of coping on little or no sleep, she realised ruefully.

His sleepy voice, a deep and husky murmur, instantly evoked a mental image of the man, black curls rumpled, dark eyes bright in the lean, handsome face with its faint hint of stubble at that hour, instinctively hurling back covers in response to the sound of the telephone to reveal a naked, lithe body with a mat of dark hair snaking from powerful chest to flat belly and strong, muscular thighs.

'It's me, Venetia. . .' Shocked and shaken by a rush of liquid desire, she stumbled into speech, thankful that he couldn't see the flame in her face or read her wanton thoughts or sense her confusion. She was deeply disturbed by the swift, sharp arousal that he had initiated with a kiss and could apparently invoke all over again with the mere sound of that black velvet voice.

'Problems?' Tyler was instantly alert.

'One or two encouraging signs, actually. Her temperature is down by two degrees and she seems to be in a natural sleep. I thought you'd like to hear some good news. . .' With an effort, Venetia crushed the vivid vision and the unwelcome longing it evoked and detailed the small progress that they had been

anxiously awaiting. 'Should I have woken you?' she
ended uncertainly, realising how little she actually had
to relay and that she had seized on the smallest of
reasons to wake him and talk to him.

'Certainly—and now that I'm awake, I'll take over
the observations and let you get some rest.'

'Good of you,' Venetia said drily, glancing at her
watch. Half-past four—and she was due on duty at
eight! 'But I'll carry on for what's left of the night,
Tyler. She's my baby, you said. I'd like to be sure she's
going to make it.'

'Just as you like. But don't hesitate to shout if you
need me for anything. In the meantime, do you think
you could rustle up some tea. . .?'

He rang off before she could protest. She fumed. He
knew that the unit nurses were much too busy for tea-
making. Did he really expect her to wait on him when
she had been up for most of the night? Arrogant devil!

But she made tea in the SCU kitchen and then
carried the tray with its two steaming cups along to the
duty surgeon's room, meaning to take her own drink
to her temporary sleeping quarters further down the
corridor in the hope of another hour of fitful dozing
before it was time for another round of observations.

Tapping lightly on the door, she opened it, half
expecting to find that Tyler had slipped back into sleep
as soon as he replaced the receiver. But he was awake,
stretched full length on the narrow bed in theatre
greens in readiness for an urgent summons, hands behind his dark head as it rested on the pillow and dark
eyes surveying her with a slight smile in their depths.

'Just what the doctor ordered,' he said softly, admiring the pale cameo of her face and the gleam of her

hair and the slender figure that the loose drape of white coat couldn't disguise.

'I wanted some myself, anyway.' Venetia defended the apparently weak compliance with a shrug of slim shoulders, ignoring the implication of the flattering words and the absurd flutter of her heart as she met his glowing eyes.

He shifted position, making room for her to sit on the side of the bed. 'Drink it before it gets cold,' he advised as casually as if the atmosphere wasn't redolent with mutual awareness. 'Relax for a few minutes and talk to me, Venetia. We don't get a lot of time to talk, do we?'

She hesitated as the charm of his smile weakened her resolve to plonk his tea on the locker and hurry away. 'There *is* something I want to discuss with you.'

'Not shop,' he stipulated, very firmly, drawing her to sit beside him with a seemingly impersonal hand.

'Oh, in that case. . .' she trailed off, shrugging.

'You've nothing to say to me, I suppose?' he finished wryly.

His hand still circled her wrist as if he had forgotten to let it go, and Venetia's heart thumped in part alarm, part excitement as the strong thumb moved over the sensitive satin of her skin in an apparently absent-minded caress. She was careful not to meet the lazily smiling eyes with their compelling, almost hypnotic glow. She had already discovered that a girl could drown in those pools of dark temptation.

Releasing his casual hold, Tyler sat up, swinging long legs to the floor in a slow, sinuous movement that instantly reminded her of another man's light-hearted reference to a panther. But the surgeon's easy, relaxed attitude as he reached for and drank some of his tea seemed to make a mockery of her momentary panic.

'There's a lot more to life than patients and procedures,' he told her lightly. 'Even someone with your degree of dedication must have other interests, and I'd like to know what they are.' He smiled at her. 'There's so much I want to know about you,' he went on softly as her feminine scent drifted across him and his body stirred as strongly as his heart at her nearness.

'Then I suggest you ask my sister.' It was a cool, crisp retort, for Venetia was acutely aware of his sexuality and fighting its dangerous attraction.

'I could, of course. But she's so much happier talking about herself, isn't she?' The dancing smile dashed the sting from the words. 'Unlike you, apparently.' He leaned to replace the half-empty cup on the locker and she instantly backed from the risk of physical contact. The expressive retreat brought a wry twist to his sensual mouth.

'It's past four o'clock in the morning!' she protested.

'So? Confidences are often exchanged in the small hours when the barriers come down and people are less on their guard. Haven't you sometimes talked half the night after an evening with friends—or after making love?'

It was said so easily that Venetia didn't know whether to be offended or foolishly flattered by the cool assumption of her sexual experience. Whichever, she had no intention of admitting that she was still a virgin. For he might suggest that it was a situation to be remedied and that he was just the man to initiate her into the world of sexual wonder.

And she might be overwhelmingly tempted to agree.

CHAPTER SIX

'At the moment, I'm talking simply to keep awake,' Venetia told him tartly. 'I'm not complaining, but I've scarcely seen my bed all night!'

Tyler smiled. 'Doesn't tally with my reputation, does it? I expect everyone's warned you that I'm usually intent on getting a lovely girl like you into bed, not keeping her out of it.' The rueful twinkle in his dark eyes faded as his body tautened on a rush of longing. 'Don't think it hasn't crossed my mind,' he added softly, brushing a strand of soft golden hair from her face with a caressing hand.

Venetia's heart throbbed with sudden alarm, but she seemed to lack the will to protest or to push his hand away as he traced the slight shadows beneath her eyes with a tender hand. Smiling, he swept her cheek and followed the curves of her mouth with that tentative, seeking touch. Mesmerised by the meaningful warmth in his gaze and his very potent sexuality, she found it impossible to thrust him away and hurry from the room as she knew she ought.

Caution and common sense were swamped by a flood of longing in heart and body as the surgeon kissed her, the merest sigh of his lips on her own at first and then gaining confidence as her mouth cravenly warmed and opened to his kiss.

It was like coming home, she thought on a stir of content as his arms went around her. She was utterly

77

incapable of resistance as his warm mouth took charge, triggering an explosion of sensation that shot liquid fire through her veins and pierced the quivering centre of her being with the sharp, sweet arrows of desire. She was filled with a strange lassitude as Tyler gently pushed her back against the pillows, nuzzling her throat with seeking lips, unfastening the buttons of her silk shirt with unsteady fingers and burying his face in her scented breasts.

As if in a dream, Venetia looked down at the dark head against her pale flesh and her hand moved of its own volition to stroke the crisp, jet curls and the strong, clean nape of his neck and then abruptly gripped his broad shoulder as she was swept with a surge of unexpected, shuddering delight.

A small, soft moan of pleasure began in her throat as her nipples hardened and thrust beneath the expert teasing of lips and tongue. His clever hands moved in urgent caress over her body and tiny darts of flame struck again and again at the very epicentre of her aroused body. Venetia was close to melting with the desperate yearning to cross an unknown threshold into a promised paradise.

In the dim recesses of her mind was the thought that she ought not to be abandoning herself so wantonly to his kisses, his caresses, his confident exploration of her body, but caution was overruled by the insistent tug of desire. Nevertheless, she managed a small protest. 'This is all wrong, Tyler. . .'

She meant the time and the place and their unromantic surroundings and the likelihood of discovery with its obvious threat to both their jobs—and the startling *suddenness* of mutual wanting.

'It's never been more right, believe me,' Tyler told her huskily, struggling with the passion that threatened to overwhelm him before he could persuade her to share it with him. For all his maturity and experience, he was trembling, as uncertain as a boy, in the face of her luminous loveliness and staggering importance. 'How can it be wrong when I've waited such a long time for you, sweetheart?'

'A matter of days!' she jeered at him on a little choke of defensive laughter that denied the stir of her heart at that endearment, so soft, so tender, a sigh of something that might almost be love if she was fool enough to think so.

'All my life.' On the quiet words that rang in her ears like a vow for the future rather than a claim for the past, Tyler kissed her again, cradling her face in strong, infinitely tender hands and smiling deeply into her incredulous eyes. Then, as passion rose in him with even more compelling force, he added urgently against the soft tremble of her lips, 'Must I go on waiting when I want you so very, very much?'

A tingle of shock and uncertainty and longing rippled through Venetia. It was a very big step and she hesitated to take it, but her senses were drugged with desire and her body seemed to be on fire, and caution was ready to fly with the wind. For why shouldn't she take and enjoy what he promised with his ardent kiss and intimate touch and powerful body? She had been sensibly, stubbornly chaste for too long, throwing herself heart and soul into her work so that she shouldn't be distracted by any man's impact on her emotions.

This eager, exciting man aroused her to peaks of

passionate wanting such as she had never known before, so why shouldn't she melt into his welcoming arms? Unable to speak or even smile in answer to his urgent persuasions, she simply put her arms about him and kissed him—and perhaps that was all that was needed, after all. . .

Venetia was startled awake by the urgent shake of her shoulder, the impatient call of her name. She blinked up at the surgeon in surprise, taking a second or two to grasp that she was not at home in her own bed but lying fully dressed on a narrow couch in a room that resembled the bleak cell of her medical student days at the Marlborough.

She sat up abruptly. 'What time is it?'

'Ten past six.'

Memories came flooding. Tyler had kissed her again, oh, so gently and with such reassuring sweetness, and drawn her to lie beside him—and that was almost the last thing she remembered! The comfort, his body warmth and her total exhaustion had combined to overcome even the strong stir of desire, she realised on a shock of dismay.

'I went to sleep!' Her fingers flew to the buttons of her shirt, the zip of her skirt, and found them fully fastened. Her white coat, badly creased and crumpled, still clung to her shoulders. Her body still seemed to be entirely her own, in spite of that fierce tumult of craving to give itself up to the promise of ecstasy, she thought on a mixture of relief and regret.

Had it all been a dream, then? His kisses and soft, stroking caresses, his gentle persuasions and her shy trembling on the verge of surrender? No more than an erotic fantasy, triggered by the weight and the warmth of him at her side? The cool inscrutability of Tyler's narrowed gaze was of no help at all when it came to supplying answers.

'I noticed,' he said drily.

Venetia's face flamed. She scrambled hastily from the bed. 'I'm so sorry. . .' It was lame, but what else could she say when there was absolutely no excuse for such insensitive behaviour?

'Not as sorry as I am.' There was the glimmer of a wry smile in the dark eyes. 'But I blame myself for bad timing. The next time such a golden opportunity comes my way, I'll make sure you haven't been up all night with one of my patients.'

'Holly. . .!' Thrusting tumbled hair from her flushed face, Venetia flew to the door, too shocked into a belated realisation of her responsibilities to heed the reassuring throb of promise in the drawled words.

Hard on her heels, Tyler restrained her headlong flight towards the swing doors of the SCU with a firm hand on her arm. 'Hold on! I've just left her. Her temperature's shot up and there are signs of internal bleeding, possibly from a slipped ligature. I'm taking her back to Theatre to investigate, and I need you to assist me. That's the only reason I woke you, Sleeping Beauty.'

'I'm glad you did. I'll go and scrub. . .'

'You've time for a cup of coffee and a shower first. The girls are still setting things up. I'll see you in the operating theatre in fifteen minutes.'

He left her on the words, consuming the length of the corridor with his long stride, and Venetia looked at his broad, departing back in dismay at the brusqueness of his tone and manner. He wasn't likely to forgive and forget such a mortal blow to his pride, and she had certainly lost all hope of supplanting Van in his affections, she mourned, as that powerful frame thrust through the swing doors.

In fact, she had endeared herself more than she knew to Tyler. It had been a few moments before he had realised that she wasn't just a passive and rather disappointing partner but was fast asleep in his arms. Torn between amusement and slightly injured pride, he had observed the thick fan of long lashes on the gently flushed cheek and the shallow breathing that scarcely lifted small, rounded breasts and felt a great, welling tide of tenderness that effectively conquered the ache of frustrated desire.

Then, he had felt content just to hold her, to marvel at the new and rather chastening effect of her on his life and to dream of making her completely his own one day. Later, he had hastily silenced the bleeping pager that threatened to disturb the sleeping girl and crept away to answer its summons.

Now, striding away from her to organise the unexpectedly essential operation on his small patient, Tyler wasn't sure if Venetia had been as astonishingly innocent of that rage of desire as she seemed or supremely indifferent to it, or simply too exhausted to stay awake.

In any case, it was a kind of compliment that she had been so relaxed, so trusting and so much at home in his arms that she had slept as soundly and as sweetly as a child. Tyler was heartened by an incident that might have damped another man's desire. To his mind, it had created a bond, a better understanding and a greater intimacy than if they had actually made love.

Working together to locate and repair the minute

tear in the pericardium that had hindered Holly's recovery, Venetia was grateful for an occasional grunt of approval from the almost-silent surgeon. Although she knew it was his style to waste few words at such times, she couldn't help feeling she was out of favour.

She comforted herself with the reminder that few men valued what they gained too easily and that it was probably better to have disappointed him and dented his pride than to have given her all so soon on an impulsive tide of wanting. But it was hard not to feel she had made a complete fool of herself.

Informed of events when he arrived some time later, Rogan Linnie looked into the operating theatre to commend their combined efforts and to check on the situation before he scrubbed for the first procedure on his list.

Knowing she would be expected to make an appearance no matter how tired or jaded she felt, and that she had another long day in front of her, Venetia was thankful to relax for a few minutes in the surgeons' rest-room once Holly had been returned to the SCU.

A sympathetic theatre nurse brought her tea and toast and some paracetamol for a thumping headache, and she sat back in a comfortable armchair in the quiet room, knowing that everyone else was busy in Theatre or on the wards and she would be undisturbed.

Venetia closed her eyes, only to find that the image of Tyler was clearly etched on her lids. He had given no indication that he recalled or regretted the deepening intimacy that had led nowhere and that made it seem even more dreamlike. Perhaps, like most dreams, it was best forgotten, for there was really no good reason to cling to the memory of a lovemaking so sweet and so sensual and so patient that sleep had over-whelmed her before it could achieve its desired end.

She supposed she ought to be thankful that nothing had happened, for she had always wanted to love the man who eventually took her across that breathless threshold. Casual sex for its own sake had never appealed to her. But Tyler Petrie *did*—far more than was comfortable or wise. It was alarming to think that she might have been as light-heartedly amoral as her sister if she had met many men with the power to bewitch her senses and cloud her judgement as he undeniably did.

'Go home,' Tyler commanded.

Venetia peeped at him from under long lashes. The registrar towered above her, springy black curls fighting the restraint of the theatre cap, mask dangling by its strings from the broad column of his neck and his powerful frame in the loose-fitting green tunic and trousers imparting a disturbing aura of masculine magnetism.

She sat up, wishing she had kept her gaze averted from that darkly handsome face and the smile that tilted her foolish heart. 'I wish I could. I'm on duty till four o'clock.'

'I'm sure the professor will excuse you, in the circumstances. He won't want you falling asleep in the middle of a procedure.' A twinkle lurked in the dark eyes as he looked down at her. 'He may not be as forgiving as I am about that kind of thing,' he added in a soft, mischievous drawl.

Venetia blushed at the reminder and wondered darkly if such a heaven-sent story would be all over Sandy's by the end of the day. For all she knew, he was the kind to kiss and tell even though the laugh was on him!

'There's very little likelihood of that happening. I'm tired, but I've more stamina than you seem to think,' she said firmly.

Concerned, frowning at the faint smudge of weariness beneath the violet eyes, Tyler impulsively crouched at the side of her chair. 'Go home and get some rest,' he urged again. 'I don't want to take a zombie out to dinner tonight. You might fall asleep over your steak.'

As he smiled into her eyes, she panicked. He was too close, too confident, confusing heart and mind and body with his nearness and his niceness. 'Aren't you taking rather a lot for granted, Mr Petrie?' she demanded brightly, taking refuge in uncharacteristic levity. 'I may have slept with you, but that doesn't mean I'm the kind of girl to accept a dinner invitation at the drop of a hat! Besides, I already have a date.' She added the lie for good measure.

There was nothing in Rogan's bland expression to show that he had overheard the flippant, rather revealing words as he strolled into the room. 'Sister tells me you aren't feeling too well, Venetia. Nothing serious, I hope?'

His arrival shattered the spell that wove an unwanted magic about her heart, and her smile held a hint of relief as well as affection as the consultant automatically reached for her wrist and scanned her face with more than professional concern in his kind grey eyes.

'It's only a headache,' she hastened to assure him. 'Nothing to worry about, Rogan.'

Tyler slowly straightened, his mobile mouth tightening and his dark eyes hardening with the conviction that Linnie was well aware that he had interrupted a tender moment and was totally unrepentant. As Venetia glanced up at the man with a sensationally sweet smile, he realised anew that the couple shared a special affinity that threatened his own hopes where she was concerned.

'Venetia did a full day's work yesterday and then spent the night observing Holly, at my request,' he pointed out brusquely. 'She's exhausted as a result and I've been trying to persuade her to go home and get some rest, without much success. Perhaps she'll listen to you.' Only genuine concern for the girl could have prompted him to enlist the consultant's aid in the matter.

'But I don't *want* to go home!' Venetia almost snapped, glowering at the surgeon, bridling at the proprietorial tone that implied she didn't know what was best for herself. 'And I do wish you'd stop treating me like some helpless creature who needs cosseting. Women can stand the pace better than most men!'

'Oh, if you're going to turn friendly concern into a sexist issue. . .' Tyler lifted broad shoulders in an impatient shrug.

The barriers had slammed back into place with a vengeance, he realised ruefully. But he didn't know if it was a deep-rooted distrust of him that nothing would ever shake or the reminder of a commitment to Linnie that sent Venetia scurrying for the safety of conflict.

It didn't escape his notice that she allowed her hand to lie in Linnie's as if it belonged to him, and a primeval jealousy stirred in his breast. For Venetia was *his* woman, *his* destiny. He knew it in his blood and in his bones. He didn't care what claim Linnie might think he had on her. It didn't stand a chance in the face of his own fierce conviction that she belonged to him, now and for ever.

Rogan looked from one stormy face to the other with perceptively narrowed eyes. It seemed to him that Petrie was in passionate pursuit and that Venetia already regretted an impulsive yielding to the man who reputedly caused havoc among Sandy's nurses. Her light words had betrayed an intimacy that caused a stir of surprise, for Rogan had believed her much too level-headed and sensible to succumb so easily to his senior registrar's rather obvious charms.

He expected that kind of thing from Van, who seemed to emerge smiling and unruffled from any number of such affairs, but Venetia had seemed intent on cementing her career as a surgeon, and he was vaguely disappointed that she had allowed herself to become emotionally involved with Petrie.

'I came along to ask if you'd care to assist with a valvotomy, Venetia. We've a split list this morning and I'm short of a surgeon on my team. But say if you don't feel up to it and I'll find someone else.' Rogan patted her hand gently and let it fall back into her lap on the words.

'I'd love to assist.' After a momentary hesitation, Venetia added impulsively, 'But on your own head be it if I'm poor company for you this evening, Rogan. I shall possibly fall asleep in the middle of dinner!' Sparkling smile and violet eyes flashed an urgent message that he couldn't fail to interpret.

Rogan smiled. 'I'll see to it that you get an early

night,' he promised, ditching a prior engagement without a qualm.

Their obvious rapport, the exchange of warm glances and the seeming innuendo of the smoothly spoken words brought a scowl to Tyler's lean face. Without another word, he strode from the rest-room, consumed with a blinding jealousy and a passionate desire to floor his blandly smiling boss with a well-aimed punch.

Rogan raised an amused eyebrow. 'What was that all about, Venetia? Has he been pestering you?'

'Oh, no!' She was surprised by a readiness to defend the man who had stalked from the room without even the mutter of a parting word. 'He suggested taking me out tonight, but I'm so busy studying for my Fellowship that I really haven't the time or the energy to get involved with anyone. I like him well enough and I didn't want to hurt his feelings, so it seemed best to say I already had a date—and you walked in at an opportune moment. He knows we're old friends.' It was poor explanation of an impulse, but she hoped he would accept it at face value. She smiled at him warmly. 'I hope you don't mind being used in a good cause?'

'Not at all—and I'll guarantee to keep you awake long enough to enjoy an excellent dinner,' he assured her promptly.

Venetia laughed and shook her head. 'Oh, that was just a ploy! I don't really expect you to take me out at a moment's notice, Rogan.'

'But I'm looking forward to it. We haven't seen very much of each other in recent months, and we really should do something to celebrate your appointment.' His hand rested briefly on her shoulder. 'I'll call for you at eight.'

It seemed to be settled, Venetia thought wryly, hurrying away to scrub for the valvotomy and hoping to acquit herself reasonably well in spite of her weariness.

In fact, she was so absorbed and so intent on doing her best that she forgot to feel tired. It was only later, sitting in at a conference about the patient with Rogan and his house surgeon, that she found it hard to concentrate, her eyelids like leaden weights, her temples beginning to throb with the return of her headache. Finally forced to admit that she needed to sleep, she agreed without argument when Rogan urged her to go home.

At such a busy time of the day, Main Hall milled with a throng of patients and porters, nurses and voluntary workers, visitors to the various wards and change-over staff. It seemed impossible to pick out any one person in that vast crowd, yet as she crossed the reception area on her way to the car park Venetia's gaze seemed instinctively and inevitably drawn to a pair of heads, one jet and one as fair as her own, that were very close together in intimate conversation.

Feeling the shock of their need for a snatched moment like a blow to her heart, she walked on, head high and suddenly clenched hands jammed into the pockets of her suit jacket, hoping to escape before she caught the eye of either her sister or the senior registrar.

No doubt they were making arrangements to meet that evening. Venetia told herself sternly that it was none of her business what they did and that it was stupid to feel hurt because of a foolish fancy for a man with a roving eye. Besides, she could scarcely blame

Tyler for going back to the sister who had first attracted him and who was so much better suited to his sensual nature.

As she hurried towards her small gold-coloured car, her face flamed at the recollection of her own response to his amorous overtures. Only a fool would have slipped into sleep when a man like Tyler held her close to his thudding heart and swept her ever closer to glorious surrender with his kisses, his murmured persuasions, she mourned bitterly. Only a fool would have rejected the unexpected gift of a second chance after thoroughly messing up the first, too!

Well, she had obviously lost him now—and perhaps that wasn't such a bad thing. For a long-cherished ambition to become a Sandy's consultant one day would surely suffer if her heart went off at a tangent in pursuit of a very different dream.

CHAPTER SEVEN

Too little blusher? Or not enough? Too much eyeliner? Was the new lipstick just the right shade or slightly too orange? Venetia surveyed herself doubtfully in the mirror of her dressing-table.

She had arranged newly washed hair in a cluster of curls banded by a ribbon that exactly matched the mint green of her dress. She had agonised for some time over what to wear, for Rogan had a critical eye. Smoothing silk fabric over the high line of breasts and the roundness of hips in feminine appraisal, she suddenly felt hot as the innocent action reminded her abruptly of Tyler's potent hands on her body, kindling urgent fire in her veins.

She couldn't seem to rid herself of his disturbing image. It was almost as if he stood behind her, his dark eyes smiling over her shoulder and into her own as they gazed out of the mirror. She could almost feel the heat of his powerful body pressed close, and shivered at the memory of his nearness and its astounding impact on her senses.

The doorbell pealed throughout the apartment, announcing Rogan's arrival, and Venetia sped to answer its summons. They were such old friends that he wouldn't make the demands on her emotions that another man threatened with the insistent tug of his sexuality. For that reason, if no other, she was looking forward to the evening.

Since her father's death, she had seen less and less of the busy consultant, but he had been a part of her life for almost as long as she could remember. Self-contained schoolboy son of family friends living abroad, Rogan had spent boarding school holidays at her Berkshire home when she was still a toddler and Van was a very new baby. As a medical student at university, he had spent long vacation with them, and she recalled a tall young man spending hours with his books on a sunlit lawn or at the mellow grand piano in the drawing-room, a remote and rather godlike figure to two admiring little girls.

Venetia was a teenager when he was a confident young surgeon on her father's firm, a regular weekend or dinner guest, so handsome and self-assured that she had been awed into a youthful crush and Van had happily practised her flirtatious wiles on him. Later, she had been warmed and flattered by Rogan's interest when he had encouraged her to think seriously about a career as a surgeon. Later still, he had applauded her progress with genuine interest and approval, occasionally wining and dining her like an older brother.

He had always been kind and supportive—and particularly so at the time of their father's sudden death, she recalled with a welling of gratitude. Now she was convinced that she had him to thank for her present job at Sandy's, with all its promise for the future. So it was small wonder that she hastily thrust all thought of Tyler to the back of her mind and went to greet Rogan with a kiss and a brightly welcoming smile.

'I've booked a table at the Firebird,' he told her as he shepherded her across the pavement to his parked car, naming the newest of the local bright lights. 'I don't know the place, but I'm assured that it's an excellent place for a night out. Good food, good wine and good service, apparently.'

And probably costs the earth, Venetia thought on a twinge of guilt. She hugged his arm and smiled up at him. 'I can't help feeling you were pressured into this,' she said ruefully.

'I can't help feeling that I'm a very lucky man to be taking you out,' Rogan returned promptly, with a glance that admired the simple elegance of her dress, the shining upswept curls that complemented the lovely face. 'You turned into a beautiful woman when I wasn't looking, Venetia.'

In fact, she had looked so much like Van at first sight that he had been startled. It had taken a second or two to realise that it was the hairstyle. He was used to seeing Venetia's bright hair tucked into a theatre cap or flowing loose on her shoulders. Van usually wore her hair up, but both sisters had the soft, feathery fringe of curls that fell across the brow, making the likeness between them even more marked.

Even without the betraying mole at the corner of Van's pretty mouth, Rogan had no trouble telling the sisters apart, having known them both for so long. Yet, just for a moment, he had seen Van as he looked down at the welcoming Venetia, and his heart had contracted with a familiar ache of longing.

Blushing, Venetia laughed off the compliment and settled herself comfortably in the passenger seat at his side. The genuine embarrassment in her manner and her innate modesty appealed to Rogan, who had little patience with women who threw out obvious lures and stopped at nothing to bind a man around with the silken strings of enchantment.

He had the kind of unwilling fascination for women that position and power apparently bestowed, and there was no shortage of them vying for his interest. He felt there were few women like the shy, unassuming Venetia in today's sexually aggressive climate. There were far too many Vans, in fact—treating love like a game and turning the fabric of society inside out with their wayward attitudes and behaviour. He was drawn to Van against his will, but he strongly disapproved of her way of life. He could never marry someone like Van—but Venetia would possibly be an ideal choice of wife for a man in his position, and only another surgeon could really appreciate the demands and the difficulties of his work.

Venetia's looks, her quiet elegance and shy, appealing femininity combined with her promise in the field of cardiac surgery had given him considerable food for thought, Rogan decided.

Venetia prepared to enjoy the evening with her handsome escort as the powerful Jaguar began to consume the miles towards the riverside restaurant. It was a sultry night after another hot day and it should be pleasant by the water, watching the glow of the sunset reflect in its shimmering surface from the brightly illumined terrace that was said to be the main attraction of the Firebird. It would be her first visit too, but she had heard some of the CSU nurses singing its praises during the week, and she looked forward to finding out if it was as nice as they had claimed.

There were plenty of women who would like to be in her shoes that evening, she knew. Rogan was much admired as well as distinguished, and his love-life was the subject of a great many rumours that never seemed to develop into anything concrete. He apparently had little time or inclination for romance, so he was probably the perfect escort for someone as dedicated to her career as herself, Venetia decided firmly. He was attractive, kind and undemanding. What did it matter that he was also unexciting?

But she wished herself anywhere but on Rogan's arm as they walked into the lavishly decorated lounge of the new restaurant to see Tyler standing at the bar, so excitingly personable in dinner jacket and black tie that her heart melted in her breast.

Observing their reflected approach in the tinted bar mirror, he swung to greet them, smiling. 'Small world,' he drawled.

'As you recommended the place so highly, I suppose I ought not to be surprised to meet you here,' Rogan returned, a trifle drily. But he shook hands warmly with his senior registrar. 'I hope you'll join us for a drink?'

Tyler beckoned to a hovering barman. 'I'm in the chair,' he said firmly. 'Whisky for you, isn't it? What would you like, Venetia?'

'Oh. . .white wine, please.' It was hard to smile, to speak as lightly as she must, to meet the dancing mischief in his eyes. Away from Sandy's, she could just about manage to forget him for a few hours. She could tell herself that he was unimportant—and almost believe it. Now, faced with the devastating impact of his smile and the caress of his deep voice as he spoke her name, Venetia knew herself to be floundering in a sea of dark, uncharted waters.

She steeled her senses to resist the pull of his powerful magnetism, telling herself sternly that the enchanting smile and the liquid lovemaking of those dark eyes were part of the stock in trade of a charmer and shouldn't be taken seriously. Polite smile pinned to her lips, scarcely speaking, she sat beside Tyler on a deep plush sofa, his muscular thigh only inches from her quivering, too aware flesh, and the warm timbres of his voice seeming to find an echo in her quickened breast.

He seemed entirely at ease, long legs crossed, one hand thrust nonchalantly into a trouser pocket and the other curved about his glass. Such a strong, well-shaped hand with its scrubbed-clean, capable air, as clever with a scalpel as at caressing a woman into eager, yearning submission. As she thought of those skilful hands on her body and the sweet fire of his kisses, it took all Venetia's resolve to keep from touching him, turning to look into his handsome face, trying to initiate a moment of the magic they had shared.

She kept her hands firmly locked in her lap and her face averted, wondering crossly how a man with so much sensitivity in his lean features could be so unaware that he was an unwelcome third as he lingered too long over his drink.

Possibly because Rogan's innate good manners wouldn't allow him to show any resentment of his registrar's presence, she decided. For he exchanged pleasantries with Tyler as if he was delighted that they had met in these glittering surroundings.

Venetia studied the scarlet and silver décor and thought it flashy, but the Firebird seemed to be a popular new venue, for several people were enjoying pre-dinner drinks in the lounge bar or on the riverside terrace and others were constantly arriving. As some newcomers appeared at the door, she noticed that Tyler shot them a swift glance, and she wondered if he was waiting for someone. Van, perhaps—or some other girl?

Rogan caught the fleeting glance too. He looked at his watch, for he had booked a table and knew they would shortly be summoned to the restaurant. 'If you're on your own, we should be delighted to have you join us for dinner, Tyler,' he said courteously, slanting an eyebrow at Venetia for approval.

Her only response was a lukewarm smile that tacitly conveyed her feeling that her escort was carrying common courtesy rather too far, and Tyler smiled, sensing the unspoken thought and almost sympathising with her chagrin. The poor girl had made it very plain that she didn't want *his* company that evening—and here was Linnie doing his best to thrust her into it!

'I know I seem to be alone, but my date had an accident to her dress and fled to the powder-room for running repairs,' he said smoothly. 'But here she comes now.'

Both men rose to their feet as Van swept across the room, cascade of bright curls framing the lively, lovely face, midnight blue dress clinging to the voluptuous curves of breast and hips and swirling about her shapely knees in a froth of layered frills. Sparkling, sure of herself, so obviously the kind of girl that men preferred to herself that Venetia found it difficult to welcome her sister with a smile.

'I've been ages. . .sorry!' Van fluttered a kiss in the direction of Tyler's cheek. 'Venetia! What a lovely surprise! Love your frock, darling!' She turned to the consultant with a particularly radiant smile. 'Rogan, I haven't seen you in years!' she exclaimed with typically extravagant exaggeration. 'How *are* you?' Having offered her cheek for his kiss, she drew him to sit down on the sofa at her side, basking in the admiration she knew she inspired in him and every other man in the room. 'Is it a party?' she demanded happily, smiling from one to the other.

'Chance encounter.' Venetia's tone damped optimism.

'No reason why we shouldn't turn it into one, is there?' Rogan's response coincided, making the disclaimer seem churlish. 'To celebrate Venetia's arrival at Sandy's.'

'Good idea,' Tyler promptly agreed.

'I think it's a marvellous idea!' Van's eager, laughing face set the seal of approval on the suggestion.

'Venetia?'

There was a lurk of mischief behind the bland enquiry that left her in no doubt that he sensed and rather enjoyed her discomfiture. 'Oh, I go along with the majority,' she said, as airily as she could for her instinctive dismay at the thought of spending the entire evening watching and listening while Van drew him deeper into her web of enchantment. Suppressing a number of unkind thoughts about her vivacious sister, she leaned to speak to her, infusing interest into her tone. 'What happened to your dress, Van? I gather you had some kind of accident. It's gorgeous, too!'

'Didn't Tyler say? One of the flounces caught in the car door. The girl in the powder-room did her best to sew it back again, but it will never be the same, I'm afraid.' Vanessa fingered the delicate fabric with a rueful shrug of slim shoulders. 'It cost me two months' wages, too.'

Tyler arced an eyebrow at the throwaway admission. 'You'll be a very expensive wife for some man one of these days,' he teased, twinkling.

'That's why I'm hunting for a wealthy husband,' retorted Van, snuggling up to Rogan and slipping her hand into his arm, laughing up at him with the full force of her coquettish charm. 'Tall, dark, handsome and very, very rich, preferably. . .'

'That let's me out on most counts.' Rogan ran a hand over fair, greying hair. The smile in his eyes belied the dry tone, for, as always, he was rapidly falling under Van's spell. He might dislike and deplore her frivolous lifestyle, but when she was close to him, as now, looking at him with dancing eyes and transmitting the undeniable appeal of her glowing sensuality, he wanted desperately to possess her, to make her his own, to whisk her away from the other men who had always been his rivals, although he refused to compete for her favours.

Away from Van, he managed to forget the wild desire and concentrate on his work to the exclusion of almost everything else. But as soon as he saw her again, the feelings returned tenfold. She had always been tantalising torment, teasing, offering and then retracting, playing a light-hearted game that promised all and gave nothing because she had never regarded him as a possible lover. She simply couldn't resist flirting with him.

It wasn't love that consumed him. If he once allowed himself to love then he wouldn't rest until he had persuaded Van to marry him, but she would be a most unsuitable wife for a man in his position. So he kept himself from loving and wished he could keep from wanting too. It wasn't love that stormed his entire being as she hugged his arm and laughed up at him, revelling in the effect that she knew she had on him, Rogan thought wearily.

It was obsession.

The tone of the evening was set from that moment, it seemed to Venetia—light-hearted but with a ripple of undercurrents and a subtle switch of partners. For her sister clung firmly to Rogan's arm and she was left to bring up the rear with Tyler as they were ushered to their table in the restaurant with its sweeping marble stairways, one leading down to the dance floor and the other to the terrace beside the river.

Tyler's hand hovered at her elbow in the lightest of guiding touches, but her whole being was acutely aware of him. The heavy beat of her heart and a rising tide of excitement mingled with alarm as she realised that he was becoming too important much too quickly.

She reminded herself sensibly that Van still had first claim to his interest in spite of that insane interlude in the early hours when they had both been swept by a storm of physical attraction that she was determined to fight even more fiercely in the future.

Venetia tried not to feel too overshadowed by her attention-seeking sister, but Van was in her element, butterflying between both men, amusing and entertaining and making Sandy's seem a whole world away— which was probably just what hard-working surgeons needed at the end of a long day. Alone, she and Rogan would probably have talked of little else but shop, she admitted, still feeling guilty that she had manoeuvred him into taking her out that evening.

As it was, she might just as well have accepted Tyler's invitation, she felt, studying him covertly, the dark good looks catching at her heart and stirring newly awakened senses. He was very tanned from his stay in Australia and the outdoor life that he apparently enjoyed in off-duty hours. Listening to the comfortable flow of conversation across the table, Venetia learned that sailing, wind-surfing, golf and riding were among his pursuits and that he was currently learning to fly— just for the hell of it, he declared with a flash of the engaging smile that lent a sensual beauty to the lean, good-looking features.

He had done some motor-racing, too, in earlier days, but that had become too dangerous a sport for a surgeon who valued his hands. He obviously liked fast cars, fast boats, fast planes—and fast women too, no doubt, Venetia thought drily. She must have been a great disappointment to him! Well, Van would certainly make it up to him—although, at the moment, she seemed to be making a determined play for Rogan, never content with the admiring attentions of just one man.

The cool, controlled and always in command consultant had gone down like a ninepin before her sister's skilfully aimed strategy, rather to Venetia's surprise, for she had always felt that Rogan disapproved of the flighty, flirtatious Van.

And, far from resenting the ripple of mutual attraction that ran through the ritual exchange of words and laughter between the couple, Tyler seemed to be actively encouraging it. In fact, observing a gleam of something very like satisfaction in his expression as Rogan swept her sister off to dance to the soft, sentimental music supplied by a very good band, Venetia had the feeling that things were working out exactly according to his devious design.

'Did you plan this?' she demanded impulsively, although the suspicion seemed to make a nonsense of her conviction that he was seriously interested in Van.

Tyler smiled. 'If I had, it wouldn't have come off. Events—and people—are too unpredictable, sweet Venetia. Left to itself, destiny manages these things very well, I've always found.' There was a special warmth in the dark eyes as he dipped his sculptured head to look into her accusing face. 'But perhaps you don't believe in destiny?'

She greeted the teasing words with a sceptical smile. 'I believe you may have given it a helping hand on this occasion! For instance, you probably knew that Rogan meant to bring me here this evening and contrived to be here when we arrived.'

'He didn't tell me his plans—and I'm not psychic,' returned Tyler.

'*Hoped*, then—having praised the place to the skies!'

'I wanted to be with you tonight and I made no secret of it,' he reminded her smoothly. 'But it wasn't *my* suggestion that we should join forces.'

'You pulled all the right strings!'

'For all the right reasons,' he said softly.

It was tacit admission that he *had* manipulated matters to some extent. Actually, things had worked out better than he had dared to hope, for he hadn't been at all sure that Linnie and Venetia would turn up at the Firebird, in spite of his glowing testimonial to its excellence. Nor had he known that Van was interested in the consultant or that the man would respond so satisfactorily to her particular brand of enticement.

'I'm not so sure about that.' Venetia studied the confident man with doubt in her violet eyes. 'I don't trust you, Tyler. I don't know what it is you want. . .'

It wasn't likely to be what she found herself increasingly wanting with all her heart. A sure and lasting commitment. Was she prepared to settle for less to please this attractive, enigmatic man?

He touched her hand, so soft and cool and wary in its instinctive retreat. 'If you stopped running away from me, you'd find out. I thought I'd made it perfectly clear, in any case. I want *you*—and I mean to have you,' he added with sudden intensity.

'And then what?'

'Hold on to you, of course.'

Venetia shook her head, not daring to believe that he could mean the soft words. 'I wonder what you said to Van to get her to help you with your devious little game,' she challenged suspiciously.

Tyler lifted a fine, dark brow. 'Your sister is playing her own game, not mine. As it happens, I've no objection if she prefers the professor to me—but maybe you feel she's poaching on your preserves?'

'You forget we've both known Rogan since we were children,' Venetia reminded him.

Tyler hadn't known that the association went back that far, in fact, and it disheartened him to realise how deeply entrenched the man must be in her affections. 'It seems to me that she still regards him as a pet playmate,' he said drily.

'Oh, Van behaves like that with every man,' Venetia returned lightly. 'It doesn't mean very much.'

'Then you don't feel your evening has been totally ruined?'

'Of course not.' She denied the implication that she was jealous, although it might not be a bad thing if he believed it to be true. For if he thought she loved Rogan, he might shrug those broad shoulders and give up the chase. As it was, every smile, every soft word, every hint of an increasingly precious interest was an invitation to love.

'Then relax and enjoy it. As they are. . .' He indicated the couple who swirled past on the low-level dance floor below them, apparently lost in the music and each other. He held out a hand to her, smiling. 'Why don't we join them?' The deep voice throbbed with compelling persuasion.

Venetia hesitated. Then she took the strong, warm hand and got to her feet and let him lead her down the wide marble steps, her heart fluttering at his touch, his smile, his endearing charm. She felt like Cinderella to his Prince Charming, she thought wildly, and let the fairy-tale magic of the moment engulf her as she went into his waiting arms.

CHAPTER EIGHT

HE HELD her against a thudding heart. 'That's better, sweetheart,' he murmured, his lips so close to her cheek that Venetia felt the rush of his warm, sweet breath stir her long lashes. 'All evening, you've smiled that tight little smile and looked away and scarcely said a word directly to me. I couldn't believe you were the same girl who kissed me so sweetly only this morning. Now I know you *are*. Welcome back!'

She drew away from him defensively. 'I'd like to forget that ever happened!' The blood stormed into her face at the mere recollection.

'I don't want to forget any part of it.' Tyler looked down at her flushed face with tenderness in his dark eyes. 'You were warm and wonderful and very sweet— and I've almost forgiven you for not following through,' he added with teasing, mischievous warmth, making light of his feelings, although he was utterly in thrall to this girl with her grave, unassuming beauty and shy femininity.

Looking into the depths of the smiling but unexpectedly serious eyes, Venetia fell instantly and completely in love.

Her heart soared on a dream of happiness that blotted out the dream of a brilliant future as a surgeon that had sustained her for so long. Suddenly Tyler was all that she had ever wanted, past, present and future.

He was her love, her life, and it was her only ambition to belong to him. For ever and ever!

Then Rogan whirled his partner to a halt beside them as the music came to an end and, at the sound of his name on Van's eager, laughing lips, Tyler promptly turned to bestow that same melting smile on her sparkling sister and the dream was shattered.

It felt like a betrayal of the promise in his embrace and his tender words. It hurt, badly. And it was all that was needed to bring Venetia back to earth from that absurd flight of fancy. The small, sharp reminder that she wasn't of any real importance to him and that most women were seen as fair game by a sensual surgeon with a surfeit of the kind of confidence that came from past success in capturing hearts.

She clutched at her pride, thankful that she hadn't made a complete fool of herself. *Her* heart wasn't really in crisis, as she had foolishly imagined, she told herself firmly. In fact, it knew exactly what it wanted—and that *wasn't* a man she couldn't trust, a man with a reputation for playing fast and loose with a number of Sandy's nurses!

She had been weak and silly, encouraging him to believe she was as wanton as her sister, but it wouldn't happen again. Tyler Petrie would discover that one woman, at least, could resist the lure of his smile and his sensuality!

Moving away from him, she reached to link arms with her sister and they mounted the marble steps together, heads close in bright, bubbling conversation that excluded the men who trailed behind them.

Heads turned to stare at the beautiful sisters. Instinctively aware of attracting attention, Van lifted her lovely head just a little higher, laughed just a little more loudly, paraded her beautiful body just a little more proudly, Tyler noticed as he followed them up the steps. Eternal Eve. But it was the lovely, slightly self-conscious Venetia with the heightened colour in her face that he wanted with all his heart, craving her touch, her kiss, her smiling assurance that she would stay beside him until the end of time.

Within moments of their return to the table, Venetia finished her wine and reached for her bag. 'It's been a lovely evening, but I think I'd like to go home now, Rogan,' she announced.

Van's face fell. 'Don't break up the party,' she pleaded. 'It isn't late and I haven't had such a good time in ages.' The way she looked at Rogan implied that he was entirely responsible for her enjoyment of the evening.

'I'm dead on my feet,' Venetia said firmly. 'It's been a long day—and night. But Tyler seems to have an inexhaustible supply of energy, and I'm sure he'll dance the rest of the night away with you if that's what you want.' A bright smile and brighter words embraced them both as she generously made her sister a gift of Tyler's sole attention for the rest of the night. 'Have fun!'

She avoided Tyler's reproachful eyes as he wished her goodnight and watched her walk away from him on Rogan's arm. Never again would she make the mistake of believing anything she saw in those glowing depths, she decided, determined to safeguard heart and body from the threat of his seductive charm.

If Rogan minded the abrupt end to his dalliance with her sister, it didn't show. He drove her home in considerate silence, while Venetia closed her eyes and pretended to doze and tried to keep from wistful wishing that it was Tyler at the wheel of the car.

If he had taken her home that night, she would have made sure he didn't leave her again, she admitted, facing up to the fierce, wanton ache of longing that he evoked. It was more than desire, a need that surpassed her body's newly awakened urges, and she doubted if any other man could ever assuage it.

She wasn't even tempted to find out in Rogan's dear and familiar embrace, she realised with some regret as the car stopped outside the apartment block where she lived and he turned to her with a smile.

As he had spent most of the evening paying court to a girl who stirred him like no other ever could, Rogan's own feelings were in similar turmoil, had Venetia but known it. He felt rather guilty about the way the evening had gone, for instance, knowing he had neglected one sister to respond to the other's tempting, teasing allure.

Yet he knew how impossible it was to trust Van's waywardness, her inexplicable changes of mood, her fickle and flirtatious nature. They were poles apart. He couldn't imagine anyone less suited to the role of lover, let alone wife, for a man like himself. But he wanted her desperately, with a yearning heart and a body that surged with hot desire whenever she was near, and he couldn't even contemplate finding ease for his longing in the arms of her apparently welcoming sister.

But Venetia was smiling at him in obviously eager expectation of the ritual goodnight kiss at least, he realised with a slight shock. Manfully stifling the persistent image of Van, he slid an arm along the back of the seat and bent his head to kiss her strikingly similar sister, his firm, cool lips lingering in the hope of firing a reluctant passion in himself.

Venetia suffered rather than enjoyed that somewhat clinical kiss—a duty kiss, she realised, more relieved than dismayed. So there was really no need to kiss him back with such misleading fervour, to twine an arm about his neck and smile into his eyes and invite him to kiss her again with the lean of her body against him.

But she did, deliberately trampling on the thought of another man, proud in her refusal to go on wanting someone who would only hurt and disappoint and eventually desert her.

She told herself she would be safe from hurt and humiliation in Rogan's protective arms. She loved him like a brother, but perhaps, if she tried very hard, those sisterly feelings could be transformed into something more suited to the present circumstances.

If she must lose her virginity, and it seemed that the time was ripe, then why shouldn't she surrender it to Rogan, who was kind and really cared about her and would truly value the gift?

'You're coming in for a coffee, I hope? It isn't so very late.'

Her smile was an invitation that no man could mistake. Or refuse, Rogan thought wryly, forbearing to point out that she had pleaded weariness before they left the Firebird.

He followed her into the apartment with its cheerful chintzes and comfortable furnishings, the feminine touches that turned the place into a home, unlike his own austere service flat, which sometimes seemed very cheerless. While Venetia made coffee in her tiny kitchen, he looked around at the familiar books and pictures and the porcelain that she had collected through the years, some of them valuable pieces that he had given her on birthdays or at Christmas.

He observed with approval the neat stack of classical CDs, for he had fostered her love of music from an early age and had often taken her to the opera or to concerts during her medical student days. They had been comfortably close then, but since he had become so successful and so busy they had seen less and less of each other.

Rogan doubted that Venetia had missed his visits or their occasional evenings out together, for she was a very self-sufficient girl and she had plenty of other friends. So it was absurd for him to be suddenly so sure she was lonely, feeling the lack of someone special to share her off-duty hours.

Selecting Vivaldi's *Four Seasons*, he slotted it into the hi-fi. The undrawn curtains at the window of the sixth-floor apartment provided a splendid view of London's brightest lights across the murk of the Thames as it flowed beneath its famous bridges, and Rogan admired it anew as the music filtered softly into the room, feeling some of the evening's tensions ebb away.

Everyone needed someone, he reminded himself. Just as he needed Van. Being with her that evening had been a mixed blessing, however, delighting him with her unexpected warmth and sweetness but tormenting him with the conviction that she would end the evening in Petrie's passionate embrace. While he was here, with a girl that he suspected of hankering to be in her sister's shoes, in spite of the surprising degree of encouragement in the way she had returned his kiss in the car.

He smiled at Venetia as she entered the room with a tray. 'I can understand why you're so reluctant to give up this place in spite of the tedious drive to and from the hospital every day,' he said lightly.

She nodded. 'It isn't just the view, although that's always a delight. It's cosy, and it's convenient too.' Venetia stifled a stab of regret that it wasn't Tyler's handsome head outlined against the night-darkened window, Tyler's tall frame dominating her small sitting-room and Tyler's dancing eyes surveying her with so much affection. She told herself sternly that it was pointless to dwell on the might-have-been and the man who no doubt had his arms about her sister at that very moment. But it wasn't easy to blot him from her mind.

'It's very pleasant.' Rogan's sweeping glance approved the comfort of the room, the attractive décor. 'You've changed the colour scheme.'

She was pleased that he'd noticed. 'Last year.' Slender hands dealt deftly with the heavy coffee-pot and delicate china cups.

He raised an eyebrow. 'Is it so long since my last visit? I didn't realise. . .'

'You've been very busy.' She sent him an under-standing smile.

'Yes. No, excuse, though, is it?' His answering smile was wry. 'I promised your father I'd keep an eye on you.'

'You've been very good,' Venetia said warmly, put-ting his coffee on the low table in front of the sofa, although he still stood at the window, surveying her with a thoughtful expression in his grey eyes. 'I owe my job to you!'

Rogan shrugged off the suggestion of gratitude. 'That isn't quite the case. I merely put in a word.'

'That was all that was needed, I imagine!'

'The work you did at the Marlborough was a much better recommendation, believe me! Professor Hutton thought very highly of you, Venetia. He was sorry to lose you.'

'He offered me an incentive to stay, but you know how ambitious I am. There's a good chance that I'll get a consultancy before I'm forty, which wouldn't have been the case if I'd stayed at the Marlborough! Besides, I've had my heart set on working at Sandy's for a very long time. Working with *you*,' she added warmly.

Rogan was dismayed by the obviously heartfelt words and the warmth of the smile that accompanied them. He hadn't realised that she was so fond of him, and he marvelled that he had been misled into believing her bowled over by his senior registrar's good looks and glib tongue.

She'd always had a soft spot for him, he recalled without conceit. There was a time when she would have been his for the taking if he had been that kind of man.

Rogan wondered why he felt so strongly that the time had come again.

'Unfortunately, I shall be leaving for York in the very near future,' he said carefully, hoping she wouldn't be devastated by the announcement of his plans. 'As you know, I'm heavily involved with the new clinic, and my co-directors want me to help them build up its reputation for specialist surgery. That means a full-time commitment on my part and my resignation from my consultancy at Sandy's.'

Venetia nodded. 'I'd heard rumours, but I wasn't sure if there was any truth in them,' she admitted. 'You haven't said anything about leaving until now.'

'I really should have mentioned it when you first talked about applying to be my junior registrar. I think I assumed that your desire to work at Sandy's sprang from your father's connections with the place. If I'd known that working with me was part of the attraction. . .' He broke off with a wry smile. 'Well, now I feel I'm letting you down, Venetia.'

His tone was so rueful that she hastened to reassure him. 'Don't! I shall have settled down nicely in the new job by the time you actually go. I'll miss you, of course,' she added with her lovely smile. 'I'll just have to make the most of you while you're still around!'

Rogan thought the bright tone cloaked a bitter disappointment. The wistful expression in her beautiful eyes caught at his heart and at his conscience, although he didn't owe her explanation or apology for the decision which took him away from her and Sandy's. Concerned, he held out his arms, and she walked into them with a soft, murmuring sigh.

He stroked her bright curls and held her close, and felt like a brother instead of the lover that she apparently wanted him to be. He thought it was just as well that he was going away, if working with him had intensified her feelings so unexpectedly.

'You can always join the staff of the new clinic once it's established,' he assured her comfortingly, feeling a trifle guilty and believing it was what she was waiting for him to suggest. It was the kind of vague promise that meant little but might reconcile her to his coming departure.

'I'll keep the offer in mind. But don't forget I've just signed a two-year contract,' Venetia reminded him, without regret. For she had no intention of leaving Sandy's when it had taken her so long to get there— and just when she had met the one man in all the world that she wanted to be near for the rest of her life!

'We shall still see each other very often, you know. I'll keep in touch. I'll miss you too.' Tilting her chin, Rogan kissed the sweet curve of her mouth and tried hard to feel less like a brother, more like a lover.

After all, he'd wasted too many years on wanting the wilful, wanton woman who would probably never enter his arms so trustingly or give her lips so lovingly. Only a fool went on wanting the teasing torment that was Van when he might forget the ceaseless hunger in the willing arms of her lovely sister.

But Van's eager, laughing face was vivid in his mind's eye as he embraced the girl who looked so much like her but who could never replace her in his heart or passions.

Venetia stiffened at the first deepening of his kiss, the first questing touch of his hand on her breast, then forced herself to accept the gentle lovemaking that she had invited with the encouragement in words and smile and kiss. She tried hard to forget the haunting image of another man, waiting for the stir, the growing excitement, the clamour of a need that would drown all her doubts. She sensed the tensing and the hardening of Rogan's body as he held and kissed her, but his rising passion left her unmoved. In fact, her whole being shrank from going through with what she had begun.

She wondered why she was so cold when once upon a time she would have given a great deal to stand in Rogan's arms, revelling in his nearness and his kiss. But she had been young then, confusing hero-worship and the dawn of romantic feelings with loving. Now, she loved him dearly—as friend and psuedo-brother, but not at all in the way that she knew she loved Tyler, much as she fought against the powerful emotion that threatened to dominate her entire life.

As Rogan held and kissed her, caressed her with almost reluctant hands, Venetia had the oddest feeling that his senior registrar was in the room with them, resenting and reproaching her treachery with the burn in his beautiful dark eyes.

She drew away slowly, easing the shoulder straps of her dishevelled dress into place, smiling at Rogan. 'I needed to forget all about patients and procedures for a few hours. It's been little else but work for months. It's been a really lovely evening. . .' Her tone, the finality of the words, left him in no doubt that it had ended as of that moment.

Rogan found it no hardship to let her go, to allow the slight, forced kindling of desire to die down. In truth, it was a relief to him that Venetia had changed her mind, for somehow, dear though she was, it just didn't feel right to be making love to her. Since boyhood, he had regarded her as a sister and taken a brotherly interest in her aims and ambitions. It would seem like a betrayal of mutual affection and the years of understanding to take her to bed.

He felt very differently about Van, however. She

had been a coquette in the pram, he thought with the tender, amused indulgence of a love that was ageless, undying and could forgive her anything, even the succession of other men that kept him from his rightful place in her heart and mind. Being a brother to Van had never crossed his mind, he thought drily. Whenever she was near, his body ignited with a flame that only she could quench, and even when weeks and sometimes months went by without their meeting, he went on thinking about her, wanting her, believing that one day she would belong to him.

Now he took Venetia's slender hand to his lips. The light kiss and the look in his eyes spoke of admiration and affection, but there was not the least hint of loving. 'I hope we'll do it again—many times. You and I. . .well, we've always been the best of friends, Venetia. There's no reason why that should ever change, is there?'

She smiled at him gratefully. The tender tone and the loving smile dispelled the little awkwardness she felt as a result of those few intimate moments that neither of them had really wanted to share. 'No reason at all,' she agreed, knowing she would be glad of his friendship in the weeks before he left Sandy's.

She might even be tempted to use it as a protective camouflage. For although she was deeply in love with Tyler, she had no intention of letting him know it or of throwing herself into his arms.

Venetia had a strong sense of self-preservation and a resolve that had carried her through all the years of hard work that had won her the job of junior registrar at Sandy's—and she was determined to protect her cherished career as well as her heart.

Tyler knew he had blundered, but he couldn't think how or when. He wasn't usually clumsy in pursuit, but Venetia wasn't just another light-hearted affair, another casual conquest, he reminded himself wryly. She was his destiny, the girl he wanted as his wife, to share his life with him. She was the first and last real love of his life—and she was doing her very best to freeze him out of existence!

Yet he had been almost home and dry. He had known it in his bones, in his blood, in the heart that had succumbed so readily to the quiet repose, the shy femininity, the touching modesty beneath the veneer of self-possession that Venetia had acquired as medical student, junior doctor and promising house surgeon in the days before he had known her.

Tyler had glimpsed the sweetness and the warmth and the honesty beneath the cool professionalism of her attitude and fallen headlong into love. Holding her in his arms at the Firebird, he had been sure that she felt just as he did. She had seemed so relaxed, warming to the music and his gentle, unhurried courtship. But perhaps it had been nothing more than a feminine desire to prove to Van and everyone else that she didn't mind the unsubtle appropriation of her escort when, in fact, she *did*.

For she had stiffened and drawn out of his arms as Linnie whirled the laughing Van to a standstill beside them, obviously delighting in his partner. Maybe Venetia didn't object to her sister's flirtatious exploits with other men but drew the line at losing her own man to her, for she had whisked Linnie from the restaurant within minutes, leaving Tyler to struggle with a fierce, hot jealousy as he visualised the man taking her home, walking into her apartment as if it was his own, pouring drinks and relaxing over small talk and a few kisses and then, possibly, taking Venetia to bed to round off the evening.

Ever since that night, whenever they met, her eyes were guarded and her manner distant. Apart from the necessary professional exchanges, the cool and quite meaningless pleasantries allowed for the benefit of patients and colleagues, she scarcely spoke to him and seemed to avoid him as much as possible.

Tyler ached for a kind word, a friendly smile, a hint of forgiveness for whatever sin he had unwittingly committed.

CHAPTER NINE

TYLER'S hands clenched in the pockets of his tweed jacket to keep from reaching out to touch the slender, white-coated girl beside him as she adjusted the special warming pad beneath Holly's small body. He had followed Venetia to the special care unit, desperate for a little of the attention that she was resolutely denying him.

'I think we can safely say that our baby is out of the woods,' he said, striving to chip away some of the ice that surrounded her.

'She's making progress, anyway.' Venetia sent him a wintry smile. *My* baby when she needs special attention day and night and *ours* when she's on the mend, she thought drily. But she forgave him, knowing that the light words concealed a genuine relief that the tide had finally turned for their small patient.

'You've put a lot of time and effort into ensuring that she does,' Tyler smiled as she lingered to cuddle and caress Holly and murmur a few words of loving encouragement. Everyone was fond of the baby who had so much fight in her tiny frame that, against all the odds, she seemed likely to survive and thrive. 'We make a good team,' he added tentatively.

Venetia shrugged. 'Just doing my job. . .' Reaching for Holly's chart, she began to write up some notes, ignoring the smile in the surgeon's dark eyes that told

her that he still hoped they could be a team off duty
too.

For days she had blocked every overture so he
shouldn't get close enough to sense how she felt about
him and undermine her resolve to keep him out of her
life, even if it was much too late to keep him out of her
heart.

She had dismissed the suggestion of praise, but they
did work well together, her interest and enthusiasm
complementing his skill and experience, and Holly
wasn't the only patient who had benefited from their
combined efforts. Working with him so closely,
Venetia had come to know a lot about Tyler—and
even more about herself. It had been quite a shock to
learn that she could be so tempted to throw six years
of ambition and hard-won achievement out of the
window for love.

Tyler leaned to stroke the baby's soft, dark curls, the
creamy cheek, and then allowed one long figure to be
clutched in a surprisingly strong grip. Small, naked
body reassuringly pink and firm and growing plump
now that the repaired heart was doing its proper job of
pumping blood through her veins at regular intervals,
a mass of tubes and wires still connecting her to various
drips and monitors as a precautionary measure, Holly
kicked and gurgled and fixed huge dark blue eyes on
Tyler's face in apparently delighted recognition.

A covert glance told Venetia that he was smiling, the
specially warm and meaningful smile that he seemed to
reserve for special people, and her heart faltered as she
recalled that she had briefly and very stupidly supposed
it enfolded her in the embrace of his love.

Until she saw him smile at Van in exactly the same way.

As they strolled from the quiet precincts of the SCU, discussing Holly's improved condition, Tyler suddenly broke off to say with his most persuasive smile, 'Shall we play truant for ten minutes? How about a coffee in the cafeteria before our chat with Mrs Garner?'

It was one more attempt to coax her into friendship at least, but even as he spoke he knew it was doomed to failure. For he saw the defensive stiffening of her slender figure, the chill that crept into her expressive eyes and the tightening of the mouth that had once moulded to his own in kindling desire.

'Surely there's no need for us both to see Mrs Garner again? I promised Rogan I'd help him with the bypass on Mr Fletcher as soon as ward rounds finished.' Venetia avoided the glowing eyes with their hint of rueful reproach. 'I need the experience, Tyler,' she added firmly, to justify her refusal to spend any longer with him than she could help, secretly thankful he didn't know what a wrench it was to rush away from the painful pleasure of being with him.

'Off you go, then. Don't keep the great man waiting.' With the light words, Tyler resigned himself to yet another disappointment.

She rounded on him with militancy in her violet eyes. 'There's no need to sneer! He *is* a great man—a great surgeon! One of the best in the country, and many people have cause to be grateful to him!'

'And I'm the first to say so,' he reminded her, mildly hurt that she apparently thought him so small-minded and depressed at the way she leapt to the man's defence. Like a woman in love. 'I admire the professor just as much as you do, Venetia—you know that.'

'I know you can't wait to step into his shoes!' Now that it was generally known that Rogan was resigning his consultancy there was a great deal of speculation about his likely successor. Tyler was tipped as hot favourite.

'I can't deny that,' he drawled, wondering how she would react if he told her it wasn't Linnie's job but Linnie's woman that he wanted more than anything in the world. He smiled at her. 'I've been doing most of the work for months. Why shouldn't I have the name as well as the game?'

He was ambitious, sure. But he felt that success would turn to ashes in his mouth if he had no chance of winning Venetia's reluctant heart. Every day, the reserved and proudly independent junior registrar seemed dearer, more important to his happiness. Every day, it seemed less likely that loving her gave him any right to share in her life.

'What happened to the Australian dream?' Venetia challenged tautly, restless fingers curving and uncurving about the stethoscope in her pocket. She was torn between the anxiety that he would go to Australia if he didn't get the consultancy here at Sandy's and the equally anxious apprehension that he would be around for a long time to tempt and torment her while she struggled to hide her longing for him—and possibly lost!

'Oh, I'm keeping that in mind, of course,' he assured her lightly. 'It's always a good thing to keep one's options open, I find.'

As he left her with his long, lithe stride and a thrust

of a powerful shoulder against a swing door, Venetia decided on a rush of painful sensitivity that the throwaway words had been a tilt at her obstinacy and a reminder that Van was a readily available option.

It was a reminder that she didn't need, having seen them together on several occasions. Last night, for instance, entering Perry's, his arm about Van's neat waist like a lover, as she drove past the wine bar on her way home.

A sudden clutch of jealousy and the blur of tears had almost caused her to drive into the back of a stalled car. It had been a shock to realise just how much it hurt to see him with another woman—and it hurt even more when that woman was her own sister.

But she was determined to keep him at bay, although it was obvious that Tyler would shortly lose all interest in her. For the moment, she was still a challenge to his sensuality, she suspected, but she didn't doubt that he was finding consolation for her coldness in Van's welcoming arms.

She had only to see him smile at a nurse, hear him speak to dietician or physiotherapist in unconsciously caressing tones or observe the swift, personalised concern for a patient that was so much a part of his attractive personality to feel that she deceived herself into supposing she could be of real importance to a light-hearted charmer, a flirt who liked women but preferred his freedom, his bachelor way of life to real and lasting commitment, if grapevine gossip had any foundation in fact.

So the best thing she could do was to get on with her job and her studies, and fall out of love as soon as she could.

'Come to help? Good.' Rogan's approval was absent, his capped head bent over his patient, as the gowned and masked Venetia joined the group of surgeons about the operating table. 'You can take over from Keith—he has a pressing engagement in the labour ward.'

'Really? It isn't just another false alarm? Jill's really producing at last?' Violet eyes above the green mask beamed delight at the expectant father who thankfully relinquished his place to step out of the glare of overhead arc lights, tugging at the strings of his gown in an agony of impatience.

'With luck, I might get there in time to see my son and heir's entry into the world, although I gather that things are happening pretty fast now that he's finally made up his mind to be born,' Keith Golding returned wryly, having had regular reports of his wife's progress through labour but unable to leave his post to be with her because a shortage of skilled surgeons meant there was no one to replace him until Venetia arrived, fresh from ward rounds.

'I'm sorry we couldn't spare you sooner. . .' Rogan's mild apology fell on deaf ears as the anxious father banged through the swing doors, almost colliding with a theatre nurse who arrived with a covered tray of newly sterilised instruments.

'The poor devil's suffering more than his wife, I think,' Howard sympathised.

'It's an anxious time for both of them. The baby's several days overdue and there's been some concern about an irregular hearbeat,' Venetia provided. She had known and liked Jill Golding when she was a ward sister at the Marlborough, before her marriage, and she had been delighted to renew the acquaintance on learning that Jill was in Sandy's pre-natal unit with complications of her pregnancy.

A scan had shown that she was expecting a boy, as the couple had hoped. Privately, Venetia felt she would rather not be told, in similar circumstances. In her experience, the pending discovery of her baby's sex sustained many a mother through the last, difficult stages of childbirth. *It's a boy*, or *You have a lovely little girl*, was always greeted with a beatific smile, whatever sex had previously been desired.

She had enjoyed the months on Obstetrics, a necessary part of her medical training, but the rewards of the work hadn't tempted her from the initial ambition to specialise in cardiac surgery. However, as she held on to a succession of retractors and irrigated the cavity and helped with the final suturing of a length of new artery into the groin of a patient who would certainly have lost his leg if surgery had been further delayed, she wondered why the driving force that had kept her going through those stressful years at the Marlborough seemed to have deserted her now that she had finally achieved her ambition to join Rogan's team of surgeons.

After all, there wasn't the satisfaction she had expected in being a Sandy's surgeon. Reality fell short of the dream, and she was troubled by vague, inexplicable yearnings for marriage and motherhood that threatened her dedication to her career. Perhaps she had stifled those natural instincts rather too well at a time when it seemed that all her friends were falling in love and getting married and having children.

'Were there any problems on the round?' Rogan

gratefully accepted the coffee she had poured for him and sank into an armchair.

'Nothing major.' Venetia spooned sugar into her own coffee, aware that the value of additional energy outweighed the problem of extra calories, and took her cup across the room. She sat down facing the consultant and smiled at him. 'Tyler seemed rather concerned about Mrs Garner. When he left me, he was going back to the ward to talk to her about possible surgery and to order some fresh tests.'

'Mrs Garner? The lady with only one good lung and mitral stenosis?' Frowning, Rogan set down his cup with a disapproving clatter. 'I've already made it clear that I'm not in favour of operating in her case.'

'She could possibly live another ten years as a result,' Venetia ventured, unconsciously quoting the argument of his senior registrar.

'My dear girl, we could possibly keep some patients alive indefinitely if we had enough organs for transplant and enough money to fund them,' Rogan said gently. 'As it is, we have too few donors and too little resources, and we can't afford to waste valuable theatre hours on hopeless cases.' Hearing the intake of her shocked breath, he smiled wryly. 'Yes, I know that sounds callous, but you must remember that we're talking about a seventy-year-old diabetic with kidney failure as well as a malfunctioning mitral valve. I can't perform miracles.'

'Oh, I know she's a poor risk for major surgery, obviously. But surely we can do something to make her more comfortable?' Venetia was surprised, rather dismayed, by his cool dismissal of a patient's urgent need of help. Was he already opting out, knowing that he would shortly be handing over responsibility for all his Sandy's cases to someone else?

'A heart-lung transplant would work wonders, no doubt,' he said drily. 'We might persuade John Knight to attempt a kidney transplant too. But even if Mrs Garner survived such traumatic surgery, which seems unlikely, we should still be left with the problem of her diabetes.'

'Which has been successfully controlled for several years!'

Rogan smiled. 'It seems you've been infected with some of Tyler's enthusiasm for lost causes!'

'He isn't suggesting anything so drastic as a transplant of any kind. Just a simple valve replacement which could make all the difference to the poor woman,' she persisted, arguing Tyler's case for him with surprising vigour. 'If he persuades her to consent to surgery, will you approve it?'

'Has he appointed you as his advocate?'

'No. I just happen to agree with him—and if I were in a position to make the decision, it's just what I would want to try too,' Venetia averred stoutly.

Rogan studied her thoughtfully. He had noticed that, while she worked hard at convincing him and everyone else that she was unimpressed by Petrie's very effective charm, she was amazingly quick to defend him from the slightest breath of criticism. 'I didn't think you agreed with Tyler on anything. In fact, I thought you didn't like the man,' he murmured slyly.

Her cheeks warmed. 'Liking doesn't come into it, surely? We agree pretty well on most things where the patients are concerned.'

'I'm glad to hear you say so. It means I shall feel

happier about leaving you to cope without my moral support. As for Tyler, shortly he won't need my say-so for any kind of surgery. He'll be making all the decisions.'

Venetia almost choked on her coffee. 'Then he's got the consultancy?'

'Did you really think that he wouldn't? He's quite the best man for the job. But I've told you in confidence, so don't mention it to anyone, not even Tyler. The board still has to confirm the appointment,' he warned.

'I won't breathe a word, of course.' Venetia was absurdly elated. Had she been fretting so much, deep down, in case Tyler took himself off to Australia and out of her life for ever? Or was she simply genuinely delighted that a dedicated and caring surgeon was to receive his just reward for all his hard work?

Whichever, it hurt to realise that it would probably be Van who helped him to celebrate.

Venetia found it hard to hug the secret to herself while her colleagues discussed Rogan's pending departure and the possible identity of his successor later that day. It was harder still when it was Tyler who voiced his hopes in her hearing.

She hadn't expected to encounter him at Diane's engagement party, or she might have pleaded an excuse not to attend. Well, she wouldn't stay long even at the risk of offending her friend, she decided.

Listening to Tyler's deep voice expounding all the changes he would bring about if he were fortunate enough to get the consultancy, she longed to reassure him, but she couldn't break her promise to Rogan. However, in only a matter of days it would be common knowledge, and she would be among those who congratulated him as if she hadn't known it in advance.

'You look like the cat that's been at the cream,' Tyler told her lightly, having caught her studying him with a kind of suppressed excitement in her violet eyes.

Venetia accepted the glass of wine that was his excuse for approaching her. 'Do I? I was only thinking about Mrs Garner,' she dissembled. Among other things, but there was no need to enlarge, she felt. 'I hear Rogan's approved the valve replacement. You must be very pleased.'

Tyler would have been better pleased if Linnie hadn't made it plain that Venetia's influence had swayed the change of heart. It seemed to him that the consultant was spending a great deal of time with his junior registrar of late, and he was beginning to despair of breaking down the barriers that Venetia had erected against himself.

'It should give her a new lease of life. I've scheduled surgery for the end of the week.' He drank a little of his beer, regarding her thoughtfully. 'I didn't expect to see you here tonight. I thought you didn't care for parties,' he reminded her slyly.

Her smile was cool. 'Diane and I were medical students together. I couldn't disappoint her.'

'I see. And I've known Mike since university. They make a grand couple. She's a very nice girl and he's one of the best.'

'Yes.' Venetia looked around the crowded room, rather pointedly. 'I don't see Van.'

'We aren't inseparable. Actually, she's on duty.' Tyler hesitated. 'I can't see Linnie,' he said deliberately, imitating her tone. 'I thought you were making the most of each other before he departs for York.'

'So we are.' Her chin tilted. 'But he had a medical dinner.'

'Then you and I must console each other,' he drawled with an imp of mischief dancing in his dark eyes.

Struggling to resist his powerful attraction for her, Venetia laughed off such an absurd suggestion and turned to Diane, who appeared at her side with a tray of food and a slightly harassed expression. 'Here, let me help! Shall I take that from you?'

'Would you? There's more in the kitchen. I knew people would descend on the food like a horde of locusts, so I prepared extra. If you wouldn't mind taking this lot over to that table. . .?'

Caught fast in the mêlée, both hands occupied with the tray of breadcrumbed chicken pieces, Venetia had to wait for a shift in the movement of the people about her before she could pass through to the table that had earlier groaned beneath plates of food.

She was conscious that Tyler was right behind her, his firm hands resting lightly on her slender waist to guide and steady her as she tried to force a passage with smiles and cheerful requests for room. Then she felt his warm lips between her shoulderblades, just where the neckline of her rather daring black lace blouse dipped to reveal a sweep of slender back almost to her waist. A lightning bolt of excitement shot down her spine in response to that lightest but most thrilling of kisses.

She almost dropped the tray as she whirled to face him with angry accusation in her violet eyes, although she was tingling from head to toe. 'If my hands weren't full, I'd slap your face for that!' she hissed in a stormy whisper, angrier with her own reaction than his audacity.

'If your hands weren't full, I wouldn't have risked it,' he assured her, twinkling, totally unrepentant. 'Sweetheart, you're beautiful when your eyes blaze with temper, but I like you so much better when they smile at me. They don't do it often enough, you know.'

Her heart caught its breath at the endearment, although common sense told her that it meant nothing. She glowered at him defensively. 'Oh, you're impossible!' she said coldly. 'You just don't seem to understand that I'm not Van! *I* object to being kissed and manhandled by all and sundry!'

His eyes hardened at the words that relegated him to a mere nothing in her life. 'Only Linnie? Is that it? No one else stands a chance with you because you're besotted with a man nearly twice your age? Well, you're wasting your time, girl! It's your sister he really wants!' He threw the harsh words at her, convinced that he was right and that she was blinding herself to the truth. 'You're just a substitute—and it's time you woke up to the fact!'

He left her, thrusting his way roughly through the press of people, pausing only to clap Mike on the shoulder and utter an obvious excuse before heading for the door.

Venetia found a place for the tray on the crowded table and set it down carefully, strangely disappointed by his sudden departure from the party and the resultant blow to hopes that she hadn't realised she was nursing.

She wasn't hurt or annoyed by his parting words, for he hadn't told her anything that she didn't already know in her heart of hearts. Men always preferred Van to herself, and why should Rogan be an exception? It didn't bother her at all.

What really bothered her was the conviction that Tyler's fierce dislike of his boss stemmed from the fact they they both wanted the same woman.

CHAPTER TEN

HAVING spent a busy morning assisting with the heart valve replacement for Mrs Garner, Venetia hung up her white coat with a sigh of relief on Friday afternoon. She was looking forward to a few days off duty, although she had no plans for them as yet, except to relax, catch up on some reading, listen to some music and watch her favourite TV programmes. She would be perfectly content with her own company, she decided, quelling the wistful thought that it could be lonely at times.

Perhaps she would invite some people for a meal. Diane and Mike, for instance. Rogan too, possibly. But he wasn't easy, she admitted, recalling past occasions when the somewhat austere consultant had failed to fit in successfully with her other guests. Venetia didn't give many dinner parties, and she liked them to go well. She knew Rogan wasn't a particularly social animal.

Nor was she, if it came to the kind of parties that her sister enjoyed so much. Venetia liked a quiet dinner, a visit to the theatre, a walk by the sea or along country lanes with a favourite person—and there hadn't been many of those in her life. She had been much too busy cementing her career.

Slipping her arms into the sleeves of her colourful jacket, she idly dreamed of driving down to the coast with Tyler for the weekend, of a romantic dinner for two, of strolling along a moonlit strand with his arm about her, of bodies fusing beneath the stars. She dreamed of the murmur of love in his deep voice, the kiss that would set the seal on a promise for a golden future, the ecstasy in a flame that consumed them both with mutual force.

She sighed. Dear, unattainable delight, she knew— and hastily crushed the fantasy and its stirring effect on her emotions as the door burst open to admit the man who had inspired it.

'Were you going home?' Tyler's sweeping glance took in the absence of a white coat, the briefcase that she was busily stuffing with books and papers.

Venetia looked at the tautly handsome face of the man who haunted her dreams, waking and sleeping, in spite of all her efforts to overcome his impact on her heart and mind and body. 'I've a feeling my plans are about to undergo a sudden change,' she said drily, already shrugging out of her jacket.

'If it isn't convenient. . .'

He was turning away on the impatient words, rebuffed by her cool attitude, when she grabbed his sleeve. 'Don't be silly, Tyler! I'm only too pleased to help if I'm needed. What is it?'

'The Golding boy.' He was brusque with concern. 'Tests indicate a hole in the heart, maybe more than one. He needs immediate surgery. I know you've been operating all morning, but I'd like you to give me a hand. The prognosis isn't good, I'm afraid.'

Venetia's heart sank. She was being as supportive of her friend as possible since Jill's critically ill baby had been rushed to the special care unit, immediately after birth. Her heart went out to all parents in such circumstances, but it came very close to home when it happened to friends.

'We can only do our best,' she said quietly.

'Let's hope that's good enough.' It was grim.

They scrubbed side by side in the annexe of the operating suite that was kept in pristine readiness for such emergencies. Tyler was silent, preoccupied with the procedure ahead of him that Venetia was outlining in her own mind as she soaped her hands. There had been a coolness between them since the night of Diane's party. Unusually for him, he was making no attempt to thaw her out—and she was still cross with him for that blunt speaking and for still seeing far too much of Van for her liking!

But personal animosity had to be thrust from her mind for the next few hours. Hole-in-the-heart babies survived more often than not, thanks to strides in surgical techniques and improved after-care, and the Golding baby was a full-term infant who stood a better chance than some newborns with a similar problem. In any case, he would be in the best possible hands, Venetia told herself with unashamed bias. She had worked with many fine surgeons, but no one quite like Tyler, whose clever, caring hands seemed to promise miracles.

A very blue baby with flaccid limbs and obvious breathing difficulties was carried into the theatre and placed gently in position on the operating trolley by his gowned and masked father. Medical ethics might prevent Keith from taking any part in a life-saving operation on his own child, but he was determined to be

present, and it seemed that Tyler didn't have the heart
to turn him out.

Venetia privately felt that Keith's place was with his
wife during the anguish of waiting. Their little boy had
been born with a serious heart defect and might not
survive the trauma of major surgery. Surely it was a
time when they should be together? But she sympathised with his agony as he stood a little distance from
the operating area, his gaze tensely fixed on the group
of surgeons as they worked on his son.

Two-thirds of the way through the procedure, the
team found themselves battling to keep the impaired
heart from failing. Sadly, this was one occasion when a
miracle eluded a determined surgeon. With a sigh and
a shake of his head, Tyler eventually stepped back
from the table, briefly covering his eyes with a spread
hand in obvious distress at his failure to resuscitate the
boy in spite of continued and concentrated effort.

Keith broke down and was led from the theatre by a
sympathetic ODA. Subdued nurses began to clear
away used instruments and soiled drapes, while
Howard soberly disconnected the ventilator and monitors and the rest of his equipment.

Choking back a sob, Venetia escaped to the deserted
scrub annexe, her heart aching for her bereaved
friends. All that renewed hope, only to be dashed!
What was the point of all the years it took to qualify as
a surgeon if one couldn't save the life of a friend's
child? she mourned, empathising with Tyler's inevitable feelings.

Stripping off his gown and thrusting it into a bin with
the fury of frustration, Tyler checked at sight of her
shaking shoulders, the bowed head in her hands. In

two strides, he was beside her, putting comforting arms about her and drawing her to sob on his shoulder, all tearful woman rather than cool-headed career girl in that moment.

Even in the midst of her genuine grief for the Goldings, Venetia knew she cried longer than she might have done for the sheer satisfaction of being in his arms.

'This is so. . .unprofessional,' she gulped at length, struggling to master the confusing mix of her emotions. 'I'm a surgeon! I should be able to cope with the disappointment of losing a patient occasionally!!'

'You're a woman, first and foremost,' Tyler told her softly. 'I'm thankful to say.' The gentle teasing of the rider brought the glimmer of a smile to her face, and there was a great deal of tenderness in his dark eyes as he dried her tears with a sterile towel, one arm still keeping her close.

Like a child, she allowed him to comfort her, to cheer her, and marvelled at the surrender of her much cherished independence along with the heart that hadn't even tried to protest but simply leapt into loving him.

He was so kind and thoughtful and caring, so patient with her obstinate pretence of indifference and so persistent in his offer of affection. How could she go on being horrid to him, denying the throb of her heart? How could she continue to refuse them both the delight they could give each other?

A nurse bustled into the room and tactfully pretended not to notice the unethical embrace between the two green-clad surgeons. Venetia hastily drew out of Tyler's warmly protective arms as the girl retreated.

'I'm sorry. I'm being silly, self-indulgent. . .'

'No, you're not. Why shouldn't you grieve for your friends? I feel for them too,' he said soberly. 'Uterine surgery was suggested when it was first suspected that something was wrong with the baby's heart, but it's such an uncertain area as yet that Jill wasn't prepared to risk it. She'll need a lot of convincing now that it wouldn't have made a scrap of difference to the outcome.' He peeped beneath the cloud of golden hair that had tumbled about her lovely face as she pulled off her theatre cap. 'Feeling better, love?'

'Yes, I'm fine.' Venetia was beginning to feel some embarrassment, however, for she had gone into his arms with very little encouragement. 'You're a kind man,' she murmured, almost beneath her breath, wondering if he could possibly entertain the slightest doubt about the way she felt about him now that the frantic tattoo of her heart had given out its unmistakable message against his chest.

Tyler shrugged off the tribute. 'I suppose I'd better clean up and then go and talk to the Goldings.' He grimaced. 'It's the part I dread, I must admit.'

'Would you like me to do it?' Venetia dreaded it too. But she could possibly enter more fully into Jill's particular pain, understanding and sympathising with the hopes and dreams that every woman entertained for her unborn child. She could put her arms about Jill too, encouraging the flow of necessary tears that she might stifle to put on a brave face for the surgeon who had done his best to no avail.

Tyler patted her shoulder. 'That's nice of you, but no—I'll do it myself, Venetia. Once I explain that there was very little chance of the boy even reaching school age and that he'd have been severely handicapped even without the cardiac problem, they might feel better about losing him now.'

'It won't be easy to persuade either of them to look upon it as a kind of blessing,' she said quietly.

'I don't expect it at this stage, naturally. But time and understanding helps people to look at things very differently. Fortunately, they have each other and will support each other in the difficult months ahead. They're very much in love, aren't they? Seeing them together makes even a hardened bachelor like myself think there might be something in this marriage business, after all.' Typically, he lightened the moment, but he was gingerly treading his way along a probably mine-strewn path.

Venetia shot him a sceptical glance. 'I'm told you value your freedom far too much even to consider it,' she returned, just as lightly, following his lead.

Tyler smiled. 'You shouldn't believe everything you hear about me, sweetheart.'

Her heart lurched, although the endearment was voiced far too flippantly to be taken seriously. It was just unfortunate that it recalled moments when he had murmured that same soft word much more meaningfully.

He studied her thoughtfully as she peeled off her gown, debating the wisdom of his next move. He decided to take the plunge. After all, the worst he could expect was another no.

'I'd really like to take you out for a meal one evening,' he said gently.

Venetia glanced over her shoulder and nodded. Somehow there was no fight left in her, no more resistance to the longing he evoked. It seemed so silly to go on treating him like a threat when it made more sense and would be much more satisfying for them to be friends. 'I'd like it too. I'm free this evening if you are.' She didn't care that her response was slightly too prompt, too eager. What was the point of any more pretence?

'Great!' Tyler made a quick recovery from the shock of unexpected success. 'I'll pick you up at your place. Seven-thirty?'

'No, don't do that!' It was an involuntary, instinctive protest, for the flat was her territory, the one place where she still felt safe from the threat of his sexuality, and his actual presence in rooms where she had so often imagined him with alarming effect might create a mutual mood that she couldn't combat.

'Too early?' He was prepared to be flexible.

She shook her head. 'Too far,' she said firmly. 'I live a long way from here and my address isn't easy to find unless you know the area well. Why don't we meet somewhere convenient to us both?'

It would be wise to rendezvous on neutral ground, and to reach it she would need her car, and that would make it unnecessary for Tyler to take her home at the end of the evening when he might expect an invitation not only into the flat but also into her bed.

One step at a time, Venetia decided sensibly.

'Whatever you say,' he agreed. 'How about the Callista? That's about halfway, isn't it?'

She blinked as he named an exclusive and very expensive nightclub in the heart of town. He was making their date seem like a celebration. 'Parking

might be a problem,' she demurred. 'I'd prefer somewhere less ritzy, too. Do you know La Campanile?'

It was an inspired suggestion, for the restaurant was
easily reached both from Sandy's and her flat and they
were both familiar with its location. Arrangements
made, Venetia turned to leave the scrub annexe.

Tyler caught her arm. 'You *will* come?' he urged,
assailed by sudden doubt, suspicious of her surprising
compliance after weeks of resistance. 'It means a lot to
me, Venetia.'

She looked into eyes that had darkened with the
intensity of his desire. 'Yes, I'll be there.' It was
important to her too. She welcomed the chance to wipe
out all the mistakes and misunderstandings and cement
a new beginning to their relationship.

Her heart sang as she stripped out of her greens and
stepped into the shower to rinse away the cling of ether
and the staleness of weariness before she went home.
She wanted to be with Tyler, not just for one evening
but for the rest of her life. She loved him. She was
grateful for the promise of happiness to be found in his
strong arms and she longed to bask in the warm, special
glow of those heart-melting eyes, even if it only
reflected a brief triumph for a sensual man before they
went their separate ways.

Her spirits were slightly damped by a painful visit to
see Jill and Keith Golding, but she had known she
must offer her love and sympathy at such a time.
Returning for her coat and briefcase, she found
Howard relaxing for a few minutes in the surgeons'
rest-room. They talked about the Goldings and the
unsuccessful attempt to cure the baby's heart defects,
and then Venetia brought a lighter note into the

conversation by saying brightly, 'I didn't get around to asking before. . .how was Pavarotti?' It was some days late, but he didn't seem to mind.

'A fantastic performance,' he enthused. 'Really magical. I'm sorry you missed it.'

'So am I.' Venetia reached for her jacket.

Howard tilted his chair so far back on its wooden heels that it seemed fated to crash, taking him with it, but he obviously had balance down to a fine art. 'You're off until Tuesday, aren't you? I suppose you've already made plans for the weekend?' It was diffident, yet optimistic, like his smile.

She hesitated. She liked the amiable anaesthetist, but she didn't want to encourage his obvious interest in her. There was really no future in it even if her emotions weren't so tangled around Tyler. 'Some. . .' she temporised.

'The professor's off to York, isn't he?' There was speculation among the CSU staff that the new junior registrar was going with him, a blend of professional and personal interests, for their friendship was noticed and discussed at length.

'So I believe.' Venetia had forgotten, in fact. 'I won't be going with him, Howard,' she said firmly, aware of the rumours that she had fostered to some extent in the hope of discouraging Tyler and disturbed that so much was being made of her relationship with Rogan by malicious tongues.

'I thought it unlikely,' he assured her comfortingly. He carefully eased the chair back on to four legs. 'I've been invited to a party tomorrow night and I'd love to take you along to meet some of my friends. Can I ring you and check if you're free?'

'Tomorrow night?' She sounded as doubtful as she felt.

'You're busy.' Howard smiled wryly. 'Just my luck!'

'Another time, perhaps.' She shouldn't give him any grounds for hope, she knew, but her smile softened the blow of the rejection.

He was as persistent as Tyler in his own way but much easier to deter, she thought thankfully as she hurried along to the lift. It was just as if Howard never quite believed he could succeed in dating her, whereas the smile in Tyler's dancing eyes left no one in doubt that he expected to get what he wanted even if it took a little time. It was that confidence, that seeming arrogance, that had originally made Venetia so determined to deny him.

But he *wasn't* arrogant or conceited or as casual in his attitudes to her sex as she had supposed at first meeting. She had misjudged him badly. It hadn't stopped her from tumbling into love with him.

She was surprisingly calm as she got ready for her first date with the man she loved. With plenty of time to spare, she dawdled in a steaming, scented bath, daydreaming, recalling every word they had ever exchanged and conjuring up the image of his handsome face and the smile that had stolen her heart.

She dried, powdered and perfumed her body and dressed it in the flimsiest and prettiest of lace underthings that she possessed. Like a bride preparing for her wedding night. Surveying herself in the mirror, modestly appraising small breasts and waist, gently rounded hips and slim, shapely legs, Venetia hoped Tyler would think her beautiful when she undressed for him. For, in spite of those earlier reservations, she knew she would end the evening with Tyler's loving arms wrapped about her. How could she resist him—and why should she want to, when she loved him so much?

First love, last love. There might be another man for her one day, but she doubted it as she brushed her newly washed hair into a shimmering frame of spun gold for her glowing face. She carefully applied just the right amount of make-up, a flutter of mascara, a touch of blusher, a murmur of lipstick to complement the pale yellow silk of a dress that had been hanging in her wardrobe for just the right occasion. This seemed to be it. Stepping into it, she drew up the long back zip and felt the cool silk shiver and settle in figure-hugging folds about her slender frame.

She felt the first clutch of excitement as she battled with the stream of rush-hour traffic that wended its way towards the coast. Drawing near her destination, she began to scan the drivers of other cars, although it was rather too early for Tyler to be en route to the restaurant.

It was some time since her last visit, so it was nice to be recognised and warmly welcomed by the beaming Italian restaurateur who felt he owed a debt of gratitude to everyone who had ever worked at the Marlborough, where his wife had overcome cancer with the help of its skilled surgeons and devoted nurses.

Ushered to a sofa in the lavish lounge and supplied with a complimentary glass of wine, Venetia settled down to wait, her heart stepping up its pace now that the moment of meeting was near, her gaze riveted on the entrance doors for the first sign of Tyler's tall figure.

The minutes slipped by until it was almost a quarter beyond the appointed hour. It wasn't like Tyler to be late, and he had been as eager as herself for this date, if for very different reasons. He would walk in shortly, full of smiling apologies, she assured herself.

Half past—and she was beginning to feel rather uncomfortable as she nursed her empty glass, looking decidedly stood up. La Campanile wasn't the kind of place where an unaccompanied woman passed without comment, and a few men looked her way with growing interest. One actually approached her with a half-smile, only to be frozen in his tracks by the ice in her expression.

If anything had detained Tyler—and that was always a possibility for a surgeon—surely he'd have got a message to her? He wasn't the kind to leave her waiting and wondering and worrying.

But perhaps he was the kind to make a date with her and then deliberately fail to turn up to punish her for a number of rebuffs.

The horrid thought popped into her head, only to be fiercely rejected. It lingered rather longer the second time. Eventually, it seemed worthy of common-sense consideration, for she had been waiting for Tyler for more than an hour and it seemed inconceivable that he would be this late—and much more likely that the recurring doubt about his intentions was well founded.

Had he forgotten all about their arrangement to meet—or decided not to bother, after all? Had he run into Van and chosen to spend the evening with *her* instead? That was an even more horrid thought!

Growing more and more uneasy, Venetia longed to slip away to the powder-room to escape the curious

stares and obvious speculation, but she was afraid Tyler
would arrive in her absence, promptly assume that *she*
hadn't kept the appointment or else hadn't bothered to
wait for him, and go away again. But how long was she
expected to wait for him, for heaven's sake? A girl had
her pride!

At ten past nine, she picked up her bag, hunted for
her car keys and stalked from the restaurant. Gino
watched her go with sorrowful eyes, and she was
thankful that he didn't voice his obvious sympathy with
her disappointment. She might have ended up crying
on *his* shoulder too!

She had made a fool of herself. She had taken Tyler
on trust, not for the first time, and this was the result!
He'd never had the slightest intention of turning up to
wine and dine her and improve matters with soft words
and sweet kisses, as she had stupidly believed.

It was all just a game to him! It had amused him to
fool her into thinking that he was still interested, cared
something for her, might even come to love her in
time. He had played her like a gullible fish—and she
was impaled on the hook of her own conceit!

Venetia was so furious with him and herself that she
didn't trust herself to drive right away. She sat at the
wheel of her small car, struggling to cool her temper
and regain her composure. Finally heading for the exit,
she saw a car so like Tyler's in shape and size and
colour turning through the restaurant gateway that her
foot automatically crashed down on the brake.

As the other car drew alongside her own, seeking a
parking space, she stuck her head through the open
window to hurl abuse at Tyler's head—and closed her
mouth abruptly in acute embarrassment as she found

herself looking into the startled eyes of a total stranger. Treading on the accelerator, she escaped as quickly as she could and headed for the sanctuary of home.

The night she had expected to share with Tyler was mostly spent in pacing the floor, drinking innumerable cups of coffee and raging at the abominable behaviour of a man she had been a fool to trust, let alone to love.

Had she really been so sure that she loved such a chauvinistic, selfish, self-centred and unfeeling bastard? Had she really made herself quite unhappy, fretting because she was torn between wanting to love him and needing to concentrate all her energies and emotions on her new job? Had she really longed for him day and night, ached to be with him and hated every moment that he apparently enjoyed in her sister's sparkling company? Then she was an idiot who deserved to be twisting and turning in bitter hurt and humiliation!

Tyler had obviously never doubted that she was his for the taking whenever he wanted—and he had shown only too plainly that he didn't really want her at all! He had set her up—and she had fallen for it like an impressionable first-year nurse!

Perhaps it was just as well that she was off duty for the next few days. By the time they met again on Tuesday morning, she might have calmed down to some extent.

In her present mood, she would probably poleaxe him!

CHAPTER ELEVEN

IT WAS stupid, Venetia knew, but she didn't dare to leave the apartment even for some essential shopping from the local supermarket in case Tyler called to see her or telephoned with a valid reason for letting her down. She desperately needed to give him the benefit of a very small doubt.

She waited all day for the call that never came. She knew his number, for he had given it to her when they were both so anxious about Holly and she might have needed to contact him in a hurry. Wild horses couldn't have dragged her to the telephone to dial it, however. It was up to Tyler to contact her with an explanation— and an apology, she told herself proudly.

Cocooned in her lonely flat, watching the pound of relentless rain against the windows and not even able to gain any comfort from her lovely view of London on such a murky day, Venetia was eventually forced to accept that he *had* deliberately ditched their date, and her heart grew as cold and as leaden as the unseasonable weather.

She tried to shake off her depression by cleaning the flat and tidying cupboards and settling down to some work on her medical books. Dutifully making notes about an intricate surgical procedure, she found her mind struggling to work on two levels at once. . .one trying to assimilate the facts she needed to know and the other insistently drawing mental pictures of Tyler's good-looking face and spellbinding smile.

She was cross that she couldn't seem to forget her hurt and chagrin for more than a few minutes at a time, and she knew she should make an effort to go out that evening or contact friends, invite someone round for supper. Diane, for instance. She hadn't seen or spoken to her since the engagement party, and it was ages since they'd had an evening together and caught up on all the news of mutual friends from Marlborough days.

But Diane's time was fully taken up by Mike these days, of course. There was no point in phoning Van. Her sister probably had a date, as usual—and might even be spending the evening with Tyler. Rogan was in York. Venetia wished she'd accepted Howard's invitation. A party was just what she needed to take her mind off a man who simply wasn't worth the amount of time she spent thinking about him, she told herself firmly. But it was much too late to contact Howard and tell him she had changed her mind.

Sunday dawned bright and sunny. Determined not to waste another moment in waiting for a telephone call that would obviously never come, Venetia drove to Sandy's to see Jill Golding, who had been kept in hospital to recover from a severe asthma attack, triggered by the shock of her baby's death. She refused to believe that the hope of running into Tyler and giving him a chance to offer an acceptable explanation had anything to do with the sudden impulse to drive halfway across London in the middle of a free weekend. She didn't even know if he would be on duty, in any case.

There was no sign of his distinctive car as she parked

and walked to the main entrance of the hospital. Denying a stab of disappointment, she noted the absence of his name from the duty board behind the big desk in Main Hall.

A porter who knew she was officially off duty teased her with being unable to keep away from the place, and she smiled, lightly agreed with him and turned away, almost wishing she had never set foot in Sandy's. The achievement of her ambition seemed to have brought her nothing but heartache.

Two nurses followed her into a lift, a staff nurse and a third-year returning to their ward after a meal break. Ignoring Venetia, who probably looked like a visitor in her lime-green suit and boldly embroidered Chinese jacket and with the flowers for Jill lying across an arm, they continued with their conversation as if she didn't exist.

'Did you hear about Tyler Petrie's accident?' the third-year suddenly thought to ask her friend.

Venetia's blood froze.

'No. What did he do? Fall out of some girl's bed?' the staff nurse riposted drily.

'That's not fair, Jo! You know he's a one-girl man!' It was amused protest.

'One girl at a time, maybe!'

Venetia felt sick with dismay as the nurses tore Tyler's reputation to shreds with the light, laughing words. She felt even more sick with alarm and apprehension.

She hurried after them as they left the lift on the second floor. 'Just a minute, Nurse! Were you serious? Has something happened to Mr Petrie?'

Both girls turned to stare at her with the slightly

supercilious attitude of some nurses to an apparent outsider. Then, either sensing her authority or deciding she must know the surgeon or she wouldn't have put the question, the third-year relented.

'He crashed his car the other night. . .about ten minutes' drive from here, apparently. But he wasn't badly hurt,' she added hastily as Venetia flinched. 'He was kept in overnight for observation and then sent home in plaster. I heard about it because I've got a friend who works in A & E,' she added helpfully.

'When was this?' Venetia tried to make it sound like casual interest, but she knew the nurses weren't deceived. 'Was it *Friday* night?'

The nurse shrugged. 'I'm not sure.'

It *must* have been, Venetia felt, hurrying to find a telephone and leaving the two girls to speculate about her identity and her interest. A car accident! Why hadn't she thought of that instead of spending almost the entire weekend ranting at his callous indifference to her feelings?

He must have been on his way to meet her at La Campanile when it happened? Why hadn't she checked instead of nursing hurt pride? What must he think of her apparent unconcern? Fortunately, she still had his telephone number tucked away in her bag!

She was flooded with relief at the sound of his deep voice on the line. 'Tyler?' she asked, unnecessarily. There was no mistaking the voice that caused her heart to throb with love and longing.

'Van?'

Venetia stifled hurt. Their voices *were* alike—and no doubt her sister was in the habit of ringing him, unlike herself. 'No, it's Venetia, actually.'

There was a slight pause and she wondered if he thought she had left it rather late to ring up and commiserate with him. Then he said hello and added, 'How are you?'

'More to the point—how are *you*?' she returned warmly.

'Then you've heard that my car had a slight disagreement with another vehicle?'

'Just,' she said drily.

'Been out of the country?'

She supposed he was teasing her with the dry words, making light-hearted reference to the failure of the grapevine to spread the word as rapidly as it usually did, but the mocking tone seemed like a reproach. 'I've been at home, hoping to hear from you,' she said, rather pointedly, seeking to remind him that she had been left in the lurch on Friday night, however unwittingly. 'I didn't know what had happened to you, Tyler.'

'Our date, do you mean? Yes, I'm sorry about that,' he said drily. 'I was—unavoidably detained.'

'You might have let me know!'

'I was rather concussed at the time, sweetheart. I did try to call you yesterday, but there was no reply.'

Venetia didn't believe him. She hadn't set foot outside the flat all day and the telephone hadn't rung once! 'I wouldn't have known anything if I hadn't decided to visit Jill Golding. I'm ringing from Sandy's, by the way. What happened to you, anyway? I don't know any details. . .'

'I ran into the back of another car. Luckily there wasn't too much damage and no one else was hurt. I've cracked a bone in my foot and wrenched my shoulder, so I'll be out of action for a few weeks. It's boring, but it might have been worse. I live in a garden flat, so at least I can hobble out to watch the flowers grow. That should pass some of the time.'

He made light of enforced inactivity, but Venetia knew how much he would hate it and how badly he must feel about heaping extra work on the already burdened shoulders of his colleagues in the CSU. Newly appointed to the consultancy and with Rogan fretting to hand over the reins, he knew it was a particularly bad time for him to be absent from the unit too.

'Do you have someone to look after you, Tyler?' Venetia realised how little she knew about the surgeon. It was possible that he lived with family or friends. He might even have a live-in girlfriend, for all she knew! 'I mean—shopping, taking clothes to the launderette, that kind of thing. . .'

'Are you applying for the vacancy?' he drawled with a smile in his tone.

Venetia laughed, relieved. 'Just let me know if there's anything I can do.' Like loving you and caring for you for the rest of my life, she added silently, hoping the warmth in her tone had said it all for her.

'I'm sure you're much too busy to be bothered with my domestic arrangements. But I appreciate your concern. Does it stretch to coming to visit me now and again? I need cheering up,' he told her, sounding far from depressed.

'What about this afternoon? After I've seen Jill?' Having made a note of his address and the directions he provided, Venetia rang off, her heart delirious with delight at the prospect of seeing him.

Come through the side door, he had said, and she found it in the high wall that surrounded a large corner house of the quiet avenue that was situated just a few minutes away from Sandy's.

Tentatively, she pushed open the discreet wooden door and entered a walled garden that was filled with the scents of summer. She followed a flagged path to the back of the rambling old house, admiring the old-fashioned plot with its massed arrays of bright flowers, its rockery, its fruit trees and the wisteria and rambler roses that camouflaged the old brick of the garden walls. It was surprisingly countrified and peaceful for a London suburb, and obviously tended by loving hands. She wondered who owned the house. Tyler had spoken as if he only rented the ground-floor flat.

He emerged from the house via open french windows as she approached, hobbling awkwardly on a plastered foot, carrying a tray that held a jug and tall, frosted glasses.

'Hi.'

'Hi.' Venetia smiled at him, heart bounding in her breast. Then she hurried to take the tray from him as he carefully negotiated the steep stone steps that led up from the paved basement area to the neatly mown lawn.

'Excuse my state of undress, won't you?' Tyler indicated the brief red shorts that were all he wore with a wry smile. 'Dressing is a little difficult for me at the moment.'

His shoulder was strapped, his arm in a sling to prevent unnecessary movement, and her trained eye detected the linger of pain in his dark eyes. She could tell from his slight embarrassment that he disliked his vulnerability. It appealed to all her womanly instincts, however, and she firmly suppressed the impulse to put her arms around him as he limped towards a shaded swing seat that had been set in the sun.

She saw the ripple of muscles in his bare, bronzed back and chest as he sank gratefully into the soft cushions. 'You're suitably attired for the weather,' she assured him lightly, setting the tray on a white patio table that stood beside the seat.

'You look cool enough in those clothes.' His glance scanned the elegant linen suit, the bold colours of the embroidered linen jacket with its Chinese dragon swirling brightly across her slender back. 'Turn round,' he ordered. Laughing, Venetia obediently did a compliant twirl, amused and rather flattered by his admiring interest. 'I love that jacket,' he approved.

'I get so tired of plain white coats,' she explained, although there was really no need to excuse her love of brightly coloured clothes.

'Your white coat is the next best thing to a suit of armour,' Tyler told her drily. 'A man can never get close to you when you're the efficient Miss Keen, career girl. You're much more approachable at the moment.' He held out a hand to her, a smile hovering about his sensual mouth. 'So how about a kiss to make the pain go away?'

Venetia bent to kiss him. It seemed the most natural thing in the world to touch her lips to his warm, welcoming mouth, to cradle his dark head briefly with a loving hand, before she sank to the seat at his side. 'Are you really in pain?' she asked, concerned.

'No.' His dark eyes twinkled. 'But do you blame me for trading on my injuries? I've seen how you are with sick people. *Much* kinder than you've ever been to me! That one kiss alone was worth all the discomfort I've suffered this weekend.'

She laughed. 'Did you need to go to such drastic lengths just for a kiss?'

'I've tried everything else!'

She kissed him again, lightly, on the cheek, an atonement for all the weeks of misjudging and maligning him, a promise that things would be very different in the future. Tyler took her hand to his lips and pressed a tender kiss into the soft palm, a smiling warmth in the eyes that met and held her own. Venetia suddenly felt very, very happy.

Like old friends, like young lovers, they sat in the warm sunshine of that Sunday afternoon, sipping ice-cold Bacardi and Cokes, enjoying the song of the birds and the drone of insects and the quiet beauty of the surroundings that were in total contrast to the clinical busyness of the hospital that was the usual background to their encounters.

Content in Tyler's company, Venetia marvelled that this was the man she had distrusted, tried so hard to dislike, while her body stirred with treacherous desire and her anxious heart dithered at the crossroads between love and career. Now she wondered why she couldn't have both.

'It was such a bloody stupid accident,' Tyler mourned when the conversation reverted to Friday night's events. 'As far as the insurance is concerned, I'm entirely to blame, of course. But the damned idiot in the other car swerved straight out from the kerb and didn't give me a chance to avoid hitting him. I guess

my mind was on other things at the time too,' he added
with a twinkling glance.

'I'm just thankful you weren't badly hurt.' She
couldn't bear to think of the agony and the anguish if
he had been killed.

'I couldn't believe it when I came round in A & E to
find myself surrounded by nurses. I cracked my head
on the windscreen, apparently, knocked myself out. . .'
He parted the fall of jet hair to show the dark bruise
on his brow. 'I was so groggy that it made sense to stay
overnight—and it wasn't until the next morning that I
remembered I was supposed to be meeting you.'

'I said a few harsh things about you when you didn't
turn up! But you have to remember that I had no way
of knowing what had happened to you,' Venetia
reminded him.

'And immediately assumed that I'd let you down
without good reason.' Tyler shook his head, not even
trying to disguise his hurt. 'I've played around in my
time, I admit, but I've always played straight, Venetia.
I wanted very much to see you that night. I hoped we
might iron out our differences.'

She smiled at him with uninhibited love in her
shining eyes. 'What differences?' she asked softly,
leaning towards him.

Tyler instantly put his good arm about her. 'If *you*
can't remember then how could I—with this huge lump
on my head?' he said promptly, and kissed the tip of
her nose, the tilt of her proud chin, the warmly smiling
mouth, delighting in her nearness and her enticing
femininity. 'I'm glad you came to see me today. You're
very nice to have around, sweetheart.'

Venetia ran light fingers over his bare chest, twined

their tips in the funnels of crisp, curling black hair, gently scratched polished nails against the warm flesh. 'It's a pity you're incapacitated,' she murmured on a mock sigh.

'What makes you so sure I am?' Rising to the challenge, he promptly swung her over him and took hungry possession of her mouth with a fire that left her in no doubt that he was fully capable of satisfying her every need, injured or not. Venetia sighed her content against his ardent lips and trailed a loving hand over strong shoulder and muscular chest and then lower to the flat, tensing belly. 'Don't tease,' Tyler said tautly as his body instantly reacted to the light, provocative touch.

'I'm not teasing. I'm seducing you,' she declared brightly, her violet eyes brimming with merriment and mischief—and something more. A promise, perhaps. She nuzzled the lobe of his ear, the warm neck, his salt-tasting shoulder. She *was* teasing, but she was also very much in earnest. She wanted him with all her heart and with all the pent-up passion that had waited so long for the right man to release it. He was so restrained, so undemanding, that she wondered if he realised that her very presence was a total surrender.

'I've never been seduced. Ought I to resist?' He laughed, entering into the spirit of the thing.

'No, you aren't fit enough. Just lie back and think of England.' Venetia stretched her slim self across him and kissed him, lightly and with love.

It was a game, makebelieve, an amusing charade that abruptly became so serious that they were both consumed with a breathless desire. Mouths locked in a tumult of longing, his hand thrusting beneath the lime-green shirt to find her eager breasts, they clung together as the convulsive flame of mutual wanting leapt higher and higher beneath the hot sun. They were lost to everything but the magic in a kiss, until Tyler groaned beneath his breath in an agony of desire.

'Oh, your poor shoulder!' Instantly, concerned, Venetia drew herself from his enfolding arms.

He smiled at her appealing naïveté. 'It isn't my shoulder. It's *you*. . .what you're doing to me,' he said wryly. He cast off the inhibiting sling with a furious impatience and gathered her close. 'I want you so much that it hurts.'

'Am I saying no?' She laid her head on his chest in a gesture of love and requited need, of willing, even eager consent to anything he might ask.

'Are you saying yes?' Tyler tilted her chin to search the slumbrous eyes and was satisfied by all that he saw in their depths. He kissed her, very tenderly. 'I think we should adjourn to the house, don't you? We don't want to shock the neighbours.'

Later, Venetia would delight in exploring his home, admiring its décor and furnishings and the personal possessions that told her even more about the man she loved. But she was so fiercely on fire for the promised ecstasy, so swept by the delirium of a love that she dared to believe he returned, that she didn't even notice her surroundings as Tyler led her by the hand into the basement flat via the french windows and across the sunny sitting-room to a cool, shadowy bedroom.

Tyler stretched full length on his bed, his gaze riveted on the slender, lovely girl as she slowly took off the embroidered coat, the slim skirt, the crisply laundered shirt, and laid each item carefully across a chair.

He wondered if she knew how much he loved her, how much she excited him with her beautiful body and the subtle scents of hair and skin, or how deeply he desired to please her and make her happy and care for her for the rest of his life.

She took her time, undressing, and he marvelled at the patience of a girl who certainly wanted him just as passionately as he wanted her. It was incredible, beyond his wildest dreams, but he had discovered that beneath the ice-cool self-possession was a warm, generous woman with a sensuality to match his own. He was thankful that his injuries were too minor to get in the way of lovemaking, so long desired, so breathlessly near.

They were still inconvenient, he fumed, longing to be the one who removed her clothes, with tender hands and many lingering caresses. This wasn't the way he had imagined it in those many fantasy moments since he had first met the lovely Venetia!

She paused in the act of unclasping the filmy lace bra. Tyler held out his hand. 'Come here, love.' His voice was husky with the need to control the raging tumult of longing.

Venetia sat on the edge of the bed and trembled at the touch of his fingers on her flesh. She wasn't shy or embarrassed before his warmly admiring gaze, but she had hesitated, for she didn't want him to suppose she made a habit of brazenly baring her body for a man's pleasure. She wondered if she should tell him she was a virgin.

Tyler eased the thin straps from her shapely

shoulders and let the delicate garment fall to the floor. He leaned to kiss the small, perfect breasts, reverently paying homage to her beauty. Then he drew her down and into his arms to kiss her, to make slow, delicious love to her with lips and tongue and exciting hands that moved slowly, sensuously and with expert sureness over her thrilled and throbbing body, knowing just how to delight and tempt her beyond bearing.

As her senses swam, Venetia shuddered in his arms and clung to him, burning with a feverish flame that consumed the last, infinitesimal shred of virginal hesitation and, with a soft sigh, welcomed the eager thrust of his lean, powerful body. If there was pain, she wasn't aware of it. There was certainly more pleasure than she had ever dreamed, and she held him, kissed him, urged him with her own surprisingly sensual response to his lovemaking, and almost swooned as he swept her with him to the highest peaks of glorious and tumultuous sensation.

He murmured something that she didn't quite catch. It might have been *You're lovely*. She didn't dare to assume that it was *I love you*, although it was what she most wanted to hear him say, in that mystical, magical moment.

CHAPTER TWELVE

WALKING on air. Venetia had heard the expression so many times but never actually experienced the sensation for herself. Now she felt as if she floated across Main Hall on her way to the CSU, and she was so happy, so filled with blissful memories of the hours she had spent with Tyler, that she was sure it must show.

She beamed happily at the porter behind the desk who wished her a cheerful good morning and at the large woman with two small, squabbling children who twined themselves around her legs and at the junior nurse who let the lift doors close in her face without even the murmur of an apology. Waiting for another lift at that most busy time of the morning, Venetia dreamed about Tyler and the wonder of loving him and the miracle of shared passion.

The room had been dark when she stirred and eased herself gently from his warm embrace. Earlier, they had kissed and talked and kissed again, like lovers since the beginning of time. They had made love again, and it had been even better, even more overwhelmingly memorable, cementing a bond that must surely link their two lives until the end of time. Then, glowing and content, they had drifted into sleep with their arms about each other.

Leaning up on an elbow, Venetia had studied the shadowed, boyishly vulnerable face of the sleeping man, wondering anew at the power and the passion and the glory of that shared lovemaking, knowing she loved him much, much more than she had believed possible. Knowing too, on a rush of gratitude, that if she never knew another moment of such joy she had certainly experienced enough in Tyler's arms for the memory to last her a lifetime.

He had opened his eyes and smiled. 'Lord, I'm hungry!'

'You're awake.' Absurdly obvious response to that most unlover-like greeting, but she had been caught gazing at him with her heart in her eyes, and she was disconcerted.

'Just about.' He had snaked an arm about her slender waist. 'Are you as clever in the kitchen as you are in the operating theatre, Miss Keen? If so, I must be the luckiest man in the world.'

'As long as there's something for me to operate on! I can't go shopping at this hour.'

'What time is it?' Awkwardly, wincing as he put weight on his wrenched shoulder, Tyler had rolled over to look at the clock beside the bed, and she had involuntarily stretched out a hand to stroke the naked, rippling back. 'Too late for you to go home,' he had announced in obvious satisfaction. 'I guess you'll just have to stay the night.'

Seeing the meaningful glow in the dark eyes that accompanied the warm words, Venetia had laughed and tapped him lightly, lovingly in reproof. 'You are utterly. . .incorrigible!'

'I think insatiable might be the word you were looking for,' he had murmured slyly, reaching for her with unmistakable intent. 'But who could get enough of you, sweetheart?'

Eluding him, smiling, she had snatched up his dres-
ing-gown, a towelling robe that completely swamped
her, and fled to forage in the spotless kitchen with its
surprisingly well-stocked fridge and cupboards.

As her life had been turned completely upside down
since meeting Tyler, it hadn't seemed strange to be
sitting down to steaks and salad and an excellent bottle
of Chablis in his company at one-thirty in the morning.
Wasn't it all part of the magic of loving that turned
night to day, showers to sunshine, a doubtful future to
a golden glow of hope?

They hadn't talked about the future, in fact, she
recalled. They had been so wrapped up in the here and
now, each other, the benison in a smile, a touch, a
kiss. There had been so many storm clouds since first
meeting. Now, their new and intimate understanding
was the crock of gold at the end of the rainbow.

They had talked, kissed, talked again, finding out so
many new things about each other, discovering how
much they had in common apart from their love of
surgery—shared dreams, ambitions, enthusiasms and
interests. They had talked into the dawn, but at last
Venetia had felt she must salvage her reputation and
had insisted on going home if only for a change of
clothes before she was due on duty. It was still officially
her long weekend, but Keith Golding had taken a few
days off to be with his wife and she had volunteered to
stand in for him.

'I'll be in touch,' Tyler had promised as they parted
with a last, lingering kiss, and she had no reason to
doubt him. As she drove across London through almost
deserted streets, the only cloud in the pearly-grey skies

of a new dawn had been his enforced absence from the CSU for a few weeks.

Now, surrounded by a swirling mass of humanity as another week began at the Alexander Memorial Hospital, it was difficult for Venetia to think of anything but the man she loved. She was helplessly in thrall, waiting with eager impatience to see Tyler again, desperately needing the reassurance in his deep voice and smiling eyes. She had no way of knowing how he felt about her. Lovemaking, endearments, his apparent enjoyment of her company were not enough unless they were accompanied by three small but so very important words.

Yet surely there had been the hint of loving in his touch and his kiss? Could any man be so tender, so caring, unless there was more to his feeling for her than mere passion? Venetia steadfastly closed her mind to the thought of the other women who must have lain in his arms and thrilled to his sensual lovemaking. Particularly Van. She didn't want to face up to the possibility that Van had been there before her, and she hoped with all her heart that it hadn't happened.

Knowing her amoral sister, she couldn't be at all sure.

As a descending lift finally reached the ground floor and its doors slid back, Venetia saw Diane's familiar face among its crowd of occupants.

Her friend paused. 'Oh, I hoped I'd run into you, Venetia! How's Van?'

'I've been meaning to ring you,' Venetia began apologetically, then broke off as the anxious tone registered. 'Van. . .?'

'No after-effects, I hope? It was a nasty business,

wasn't it? I hear the car was a virtual write-off. I'd finally gone off duty, but I heard all about it the next day. A & E was buzzing, as you can imagine, seeing that the hospital heart-throb was involved! The juniors were green with envy, but it wouldn't have seemed so romantic if Tyler Petrie or Van had been badly hurt in that accident, would it? They were both very lucky. You must be relieved that Van got out without a scratch. But she shouldn't have insisted on going home that night, nevertheless.'

Her blood turned to ice, Venetia's brain was obstinately refusing to make any sense of the battering flow of words. How could she believe what she was hearing? That *Van* had been in Tyler's car at the time of the accident? Late at night? When he should have been with *her* at La Campanile?

'Yes—yes, it was lucky,' she managed to stammer, forcing a stiff smile. 'I'm sorry, I must rush, Diane— I'm dreadfully late. I'll talk to you later. . .'

Blindly, she allowed herself to be swept into the lift by an impatient surge of nurses going on duty. Deaf to everything but the echoing concern in the Casualty Officer's lilting voice, she stood in the crowded confines and was carried up to the SCU floor. She was unaware of being addressed by, or of answering to, any member of the unit staff as she blindly walked like an automaton, feet as leaden as her heart, along the corridor to the changing-rooms.

Why hadn't she known? Why hadn't Tyler told her that Van was involved in that accident? Why had he allowed her to go on believing he was on his way to meet *her* when the accident took place?

The answer seemed obvious. How relieved he must

have been that she plainly had no idea he had ditched her on Friday evening to be with her sister!

Venetia shuddered from head to toe, recalling the hours she had spent in bed with the sensual surgeon, bitterly regretting not only the gift of her precious virginity but also the much more precious gift of her love to a man who simply wasn't worth it, after all. He was just an opportunist—and he'd certainly made the most of the opportunity she had offered by rushing to see him with such betraying concern as soon as she learned that he'd been hurt in that car crash!

He wasn't entirely to blame, however, she admitted fairly. Like some naïve junior nurse, she had fallen for his charm—hook, line and sinker!

Reaching for a telephone, she dialled the number of Elizabeth Ward and asked to speak to her sister. It was high time she showed some sisterly concern—and berated Van for leaving her so utterly in the dark. Not only about being in Tyler's car with him when it crashed but also about the extent of her involvement with the man!

Staff Nurse Keen was off duty until the following morning, she was told. 'Thank you, Sister.' There was no reply from Van's home number, and Venetia replaced the receiver with a cold band of dread about her heart.

There was no need to wonder where Van might be, she decided on a surge of bitter jealousy. Obviously she was with Tyler, consoling him for the pain in his shoulder, his injured foot, the trauma of the accident. Just as *she* had! Van and herself were probably turn-and-turn-about lovers for a man without heart, conscience or a shred of integrity!

Hadn't she suspected from the very beginning that he was the kind to enjoy the pursuit and conquest of both herself and her look-alike sister? He was the last man in the world that she should have allowed herself to love!

Well, she would get over it—eventually. In the meantime, there was plenty of work to occupy mind and hands and cure a grieving heart. Falling in love with Tyler Petrie had been a salutary lesson. She had learned that a girl could be so blinded by dreams of a future as a brilliant surgeon that she didn't see the present danger in a man's smiling attentions. It wouldn't happen again!

Van was welcome to him, she thought proudly. For her part, she would be glad if she never saw Tyler Petrie again—and she said so, more or less, when he rang her later in the day.

At first, Venetia was tempted to refuse to take the call that came in the middle of an Outpatients Clinic. But there was no point in putting off what had to be said. 'Venetia Keen speaking. . .what can I do for you?' The distant tone and the deliberate formality was a verbal slap in the face for a man who must know that she had been informed of the identity of her caller.

'It's me, sweetheart.'

She hardened her heart to withstand the melting seduction of the familiar endearment, said as only he could say it. 'This isn't very convenient, Tyler. I'm up to my eyes in patients. Rogan isn't back from York and. . .'

'And I'm lazing in the sun when I'm most needed,' he finished wryly. 'I know you must be busy, and I won't keep you more than a few minutes. I just wanted to know how you are.'

'How should I be?'

The caressing warmth of his deep voice had implied an ache of longing that could only be eased by talking to her—and then only until he saw her again. He was a charmer with all the weapons of attraction and experience at his command, she thought bitterly.

'*Ouch*!' Untroubled amusement lilted in the exclamation that greeted her snubbing reply. 'You *are* in a crocodile mood this afternoon! You must be missing me.'

'Not in the least,' said Venetia coldly.

'Much too busy, I suppose? While I've nothing to do but think about you and wait for tonight. You *are* coming to. . .cook my supper for me again, aren't you?'

The coaxing words with their subtle innuendo brought a burn to Venetia's cheeks. 'Not tonight or any other night,' she told him crisply with blunt, unmistakable rejection.

The ice in her tone had finally got through to him and a momentary silence greeted her words. Then he said quietly, 'That sounds very final. It's a sudden change of heart, isn't it?'

He sounded shocked, hurt. Venetia steeled herself to think only of her own shock and dismay and humiliated heart. 'Perhaps I've a very good reason.'

'Perhaps you'd like to explain it to me.' It was a command rather than a suggestion, a hint of the steel that was never far from the surface and was part of his potent attraction. 'Oh, not now—you're busy. But we need to talk—soon! I'm not letting you go that easily, Venetia. I l——'

She put down the phone, abruptly, cutting off whatever he had been about to say. There was nothing he *could* say to coax her back into his arms. She would never trust him again!

She nodded at the nurse who hovered at the door of the examination-room and had probably heard her side of the telephone conversation. She couldn't remember if she had used Tyler's name at any time, but no doubt she had. Something more for the juniors to gossip about—but that was only one of the hazards of working in a large general hospital. Everyone assumed that romance must be rife between members of the staff!

'I'll have the next patient in now, please, Nurse.'

It wasn't easy for Venetia to keep her mind on her work, to smile and ask the right questions as she examined the anxious woman, to make reassuring noises while she arranged for a number of tests and a further appointment. The patient would need to be seen by Rogan or his successor before a decision could be made about treatment or possible surgery for an obviously impaired heart.

Her own heart was badly bruised and in need of radical surgery to cure its foolish response to a very dangerous charm, Venetia thought heavily. Perhaps *she* ought to consult Rogan, who was so expert at dealing with heart problems.

'Mr Linnie's here.'

Some time later, Venetia looked round at the sister who put her head round the door with the welcome news. 'Oh, good! Would you tell him I'd like a word?'

He was very late, but at least he had arrived while the Cardiac Clinic was still in progress. There were several queries about patients seen in his absence that she wanted to discuss with him.

Between patients, she slipped through the communicating door between consulting-rooms. Rogan was reading a referral letter from a GP before seeing a new patient, but he instantly laid it down and smiled at her in warm welcome.

'I'm sorry you were left to hold the fort virtually single-handed this afternoon. Contraflow on the motorway causing the usual problems, I'm afraid.' It wasn't the sole cause of his lateness, but it sufficed, he felt.

'Oh, we've coped,' Venetia assured him modestly.

He nodded. 'Of course you have.'

His tone spoke of so much confidence in her, so much affection for her, that Venetia's heart welled and then jumped at a possible solution to the problem of successfully impressing on Tyler that a very brief idyll had come to an end. She put the idea to the back of her mind until a more suitable moment for consideration.

'It's been a particularly busy clinic, because we've had to manage without Tyler too. I suppose you know he had an accident at the weekend?' She forced herself to say his name without flinching.

'Oh, I heard all about that, of course,' Rogan agreed. 'Damned inconvenient, but it could have been worse. He should be fit enough to take over from me at the end of the month, and I've put off my departure until then. We're having one or two problems with the official opening of the Laurence Keen Clinic, so it all works out reasonably well.' He smiled at her, anticipating her reaction.

Venetia stared in delighted surprise. 'The Laurence Keen Clinic?' she echoed. 'Is that really the name of the new venture? I'm so pleased!' She almost threw her arms about him. Only the entrance of Sister Merridew at that moment deterred her from expressing her pleasure in such an unconventional manner.

'I thought you'd like it,' Rogan said mildly, surveying her with a degree of satisfaction in his grey eyes. He owed so much to her father that he'd been glad of the chance to pay lasting tribute to the memory of the famous surgeon, but he had been waiting for the official seal of approval from co-founders and fellow-directors before making the announcement. Venetia's response was all that he had hoped. Van had been disappointingly unmoved.

'Oh, I do—very much! It's just the appreciation of his work that he'd have liked!' Warmed by the generous gesture, Venetia wondered how she could show her gratitude—and an earlier impulse came to mind.

She had half-heartedly used Rogan as camouflage ever since she had realised that her feeling for his senior registrar was leading her into uncharted waters. Now she decided to encourage him to play a really prominent part in her life. They had always been very good friends. There was no reason why they shouldn't eventually become lovers, she decided defiantly, recalling the way he had held and kissed her and smiled into her eyes on an eventful night.

Allowing him into her arms might stamp out the memory of the ecstasy she had shared with Tyler, and surely she could learn to care for him enough to snuff the candle in her heart that burned so brightly for another man? Particularly if she ensured that Tyler and herself were miles apart.

Sandy's was something of a disappointment, after all. So why shouldn't she go to York with Rogan and help him to make a success of the new clinic? Put everything behind her, including the futility of loving, and make a new start in a new place, with Rogan's support? He had already suggested it, she reminded herself.

She glanced at the girl in the dark blue dress and starched organza cap who was fiddling with a stack of forms at the other side of the room but must be listening to every word. 'I know you've got patients waiting to see you, but can you spare a few minutes for a private word?' she ventured.

Instantly, the consultant swivelled in his chair. 'Sister, I can't find the report on Mr Hamilton's recent EEG in the file. Could you chase it up—and tell him I won't keep him waiting very much longer?'

'Yes, of course, Professor Linnie.' She went from the room, not quite closing the door. Venetia walked across and shut it firmly.

Rogan leaned back in the chair to study the slim girl in the long white coat with her pale, grave face and earnest eyes, and wondered what was so important that it couldn't wait until the end of Clinic. She was beautiful, with an austere, touch-me-not coolness of looks and personality that some men would see as a challenge, he knew.

His pulses only seemed to quicken for her extrovert, exciting sister. Van was a bright flame, a joy and a delight, irresistible temptation even when a man knew he would burn his fingers and singe his heart, Rogan thought wryly, knowing he would dare anything, risk anything, be anything for one short hour with a woman he loved with all his heart and soul.

But she was so flippant, so fickle and so faithless by nature that he had absolutely no idea what the future held, and it seemed painfully inevitable that she regarded him as just one more man in her life, soon to be discarded. Common sense told him there was no other likely or suitable ending for something he should never have begun. But what did common sense have to do with the passionate obsession with wilful, wanton, utterly wonderful Van?

He loved her so much that he had even forgiven her for laughing when he asked her to marry him.

'I've been thinking, Rogan. . .'

The hesitant words dragged his thoughts from the tantalising image of her wayward sister. He smiled encouragement. 'Go on.'

'I want to come to York with you,' Venetia declared breathlessly, plunging in before second thoughts weakened the new resolve. 'When you leave at the end of the month, I mean! You can pull strings to get me released from my contract. I'm only a junior registrar, easily enough replaced.'

'Do you really want to do that? Give up all you've worked for? So soon? You haven't given Sandy's much of a chance, have you?' Taken by surprise, Rogan played for time, wondering what prompted the words. Did she know about him and Van? Was she so upset, so jealous, that she made the decision to leave with an uncharacteristic haste and urgency?

'There isn't any point in being here if you're miles

away in York. I want to be where you are, Rogan. It's what I've always wanted.' She was blatantly throwing herself at him, and it was to his credit that he didn't show the dismay that he possibly felt. 'I'd never have applied for the job here at Sandy's if I'd known you were leaving!'

'I feel rather guilty about that,' Rogan admitted, thoroughly shaken. 'You had excellent career prospects at the Marlborough.' He had believed her to be caught up in a vortex of feeling for Petrie, and it was a shock to learn that she was as obsessed with him as he was with Van—and he didn't quite know how to deal with the situation. It had been so much easier when she was seventeen! 'I had no idea you felt so strongly about working with me. I thought the object was to follow in your father's footsteps.'

Venetia smiled at him. 'For such a clever man, you can be very stupid at times,' she said gently. 'Do I really have to spell it out for you, Rogan?' She neatly avoided uttering an outright lie about loving him. He could make what he liked of her words, her behaviour, as long as he provided her with an honourable excape from the almost daily torment of working with a man who didn't love her.

Rogan felt as if he was being backed into a corner. At the same time, her obvious affection for him was balm for a heart that burned from the callous rejection handed out by her sister. He shrank from calling it love. 'I'll do what I can for you, of course. I can promise you a job—no problem! But it may not be easy to get your contract cancelled. The Board won't like it, Venetia. No extenuating circumstances, you see.'

'Tell them we're going to be married.'

Her smile was so spontaneous, so incandescent, that for a glowing moment she was the image of Van. For as long as it took to breathe in and out, Rogan toyed with the idea of actually taking her up on the impossible suggestion. . .

CHAPTER THIRTEEN

WORD spread like a forest fire. The grapevine had branches in every ward, every department at Sandy's—and it was shock news! *Rogan Linnie and his new junior registrar were getting married*!

It was gospel truth, junior nurses insisted to doubting colleagues. Sister Merridew had heard the consultant actually asking Miss Keen to marry him when she inadvertently walked in on them—right in the middle of the Cardiac Clinic! Telephone lines were red-hot as nurses broke hospital rules to ring friends who were off duty or working on other wards. Huddles of excited staff gossiped avidly about the distinguished surgeon who had always seemed such a cold fish. No wonder he had taken a woman on to his surgical firm for the very first time—she was his girlfriend!

He'd loved her for years and she'd insisted on putting career before love, but he'd finally worn her down, the romantics happily declared. It was just what Sandy's nurses most enjoyed, an unsuspected love affair going on under their very noses!

Unaware of all the excitement that rippled along corridors and down wards and through the SCU, Venetia saw the rest of the patients allotted to her and tried not to think about the humiliation she had brought upon herself.

Poor Rogan hadn't bargained for that assault on his

good nature. Fortunately, he was too expert at wriggling out of unwanted predicaments to be pressured into a pretend engagement, she thought thankfully, her cheeks flaming as she recalled that her half-in-earnest words had rung across the room as Sister Merridew walked in, flourishing the missing EEG result.

'The report you wanted, Professor Linnie. . .' She was much too well trained to show if she had overheard the foolish words or what she made of them.

Rogan had turned on her, nearer to anger than Venetia had ever seen him, a chill in eyes and tone as he snapped, 'I'll buzz when I'm ready for my patient, Sister.' The girl had hastily backed from the room, but Venetia fancied she had taken in the situation at a glance, quite incorrectly. 'I wish those girls would knock occasionally.' Anger subsiding, Rogan had continued evenly, 'The Board might accept that as a reason for your resignation, but I don't think we need to go to those lengths, do we?'

It was lightly said, but the absence of a smile in the grey eyes spoke volumes. 'It was just a joke,' Venetia had stumbled, feeling sick with embarrassment, thankful he hadn't taken her seriously.

He had nodded. Then, softening, he got to his feet and put his hands on her shoulders to look down at her with the warm kindliness and understanding that she had always associated with him. 'Don't rush into anything, Venetia. Take my advice and stay where you are for the time being. York really doesn't have very much to offer you.'

Letting her down gently, she'd instantly known, and marvelled that it was so easy to convey love for him when her heart hungered so desperately for another man.

Were all men so conceited, so sure of their desirability as lovers and husbands, so convinced that they had only to pay a woman some small attention for her to fall head over heels in love? Not that Tyler had expected or wanted her to love him, she conceded fairly. He had only seen her as a temporary distraction, a reward for the demands and long hours and grim dedication of his job, another name in his little black book—along with that of her sister.

She couldn't blame Rogan either. She had been utterly brazen in her approach—and clumsy too. Van would have managed things so much better.

Venetia was unaware of curious glances and the way that conversations broke off at her approach as she left the Clinic later that afternoon, or she might have wondered if Sister Merridew had indiscreetly repeated an overheard remark and spread false rumours that would embarrass both herself and Rogan.

She was thankful to be going off duty, needing to be alone to come to terms with the collapse of a dream that had stupidly centred on the wrong man. She should have fallen in love with Rogan, for she would have stood a better chance of capturing *his* heart, and she could have trusted him not to use her, hurt her, let her down so badly by blatantly preferring her sister.

Rogan had never really liked or approved of Van.

'Venetia!'

Ascending the stone stairway that led to the SCU, on her way to collect her things before heading for home, Venetia turned in surprise at the unexpected sound of her sister's voice. She was about to smile when she remembered that she had good reason to feel angry, betrayed.

'I thought you were off duty,' she said.

'I am.' Hotfoot from home after a telephone call from a friend on Elizabeth Ward who thought she'd be interested in the latest piece of gossip, Van was in no mood to waste words. She had laughingly dismissed something so unlikely until Maggie had insisted it was true, and then she had never felt less like laughing in her life—or more threatened. 'I guess you found out what happened this weekend?' she challenged.

Venetia wondered why she had expected contrition. Van must sense her hurt, her anger, but there wasn't even a hint of regret or apology in her tone. In fact, it was just like her to defend her own wilful behaviour with attack, she thought bitterly. 'Did you think I wouldn't?' she asked coldly.

Van shrugged. 'It didn't bother me one way or the other, frankly. I didn't think you cared that much about him. If you'd told me I was poaching, I'd have left him alone.' At least she'd have *tried*. She hadn't planned this. What had happened had just. . . *happened*—and no one could be more surprised than herself!

'I don't think you could leave any man alone. Particularly if you thought he was interested in *me*!' The resentment that had smouldered for years suddenly surged to the surface.

It wasn't the first time that Van had done this to her! She always had to prove that she was the prettier, the more popular, the sister that every man preferred to the other! Tyler, like every other man, had been so ensnared in the web of Van's enchantment that everything he had ever said to *her*, every smile, every touch, every kiss and caress, had been a lie. Venetia was deeply, bitterly hurt—and her own sister had compounded the injury!

'Harking back to Paul?' Van sounded unrepentant, but the way she read her sister's mind proved that she had always felt a little guilty about that long-ago incident. 'He was an awful wet—and he never really wanted *you*, anyway. You were too much of an iceberg,' she swept on bluntly. 'It was the same this time, if you must have the truth.' She was fighting for something that she hadn't known she wanted until it seemed about to slip away from her—and she didn't care what weapons she used or if she damaged her relationship with her sister beyond repair. 'You can't give him what he wants. I *can*!'

'You've certainly had enough practice,' Venetia said stonily, a brutal hand gripping her heart as she realised that Tyler must have compared their responses in bed—and told Van she was more to his liking!

Could the man who had held her so tenderly, kissed her so lovingly, be so entirely without heart or conscience? It seemed so—and that proved just how little she knew about men and just how instinctively right she had been to avoid tangling with them in the past!

Van stiffened. She didn't need reminding of the many men in her past. 'I don't want to quarrel with you, but I'm not letting you have him. He means too much to me,' she said carefully, so quietly that it was convincing. 'I didn't know *how* much until this weekend. Now. . .well, I don't know what he's been saying to you, but he asked *me* to marry him—and he meant it. I know he did!'

Venetia put a hand to the iron stair-rail to steady herself as dismay and a drowning despair swept over her. 'And is that what you want?' She forced out the words.

'Yes, it is. I'm going to see him right now to straighten things out. . .' A couple of medical students in the inevitable tweed jackets had mounted the stairs, and as they came level, Van's bright, confident smile embraced both her sister and the two men alike as she turned to hasten back the way she had come.

Having left Venetia in no doubt of the situation, as she supposed, she was hurrying to secure her future— and nothing was going to stand in the way of her happiness. It had taken much too long to discover where it lay!

She couldn't allow herself to feel sorry for her obviously stricken sister. Venetia could have snapped him up at any time, after all, and if she had lost him because she couldn't choose between love and her precious career then that was her own fault. While Van had always known what she really wanted, even if the man who figured in her dream of marriage and happy ever after had been shadowy and unreal until now.

Rogan had always seemed so remote, so unmoved, merely humouring her flirtatious assaults on his apparently impenetrable heart. So she had been surprised and delighted when he suggested the weekend in York, and his proposal of marriage during those incredibly happy few days had been so unexpected, so breathtaking, that she had answered him with a nervous laugh and a stupid joke, lost for words for the first time in her life. Now she was about to make amends and tell him *yes*—and that would promtly put paid to the absurd rumour that had him engaged to the wrong Miss Keen!

Venetia allowed the students to pass her with a perfunctory smile, a pale shadow of the one her sister had bestowed on them, feeling shattered and breathless with shock. The last vestige of hope had died with Van's confident words. No one could be more determined than her sister, and since infancy she had stretched out greedy hands to take whatever she wanted.

She seemed to inspire love in any man she chose and she had the lightest of touches when it came to relationships. Venetia, serious, steady and rather shy, had stifled her emotional needs for so long that she had no idea how to cope when love exploded like a thunderbolt into her life.

Her startled heart had gone into crisis and, hopelessly at a loss, she had said and done all the wrong things and lost the only man she would ever love.

The man who was apparently hoping to become her brother-in-law.

Unable to face anyone for the time being, Venetia dodged the hovering Howard and slipped past the surgeons' rest-room and avoided Main Hall, leaving the hospital by a side door and scurrying to her parked car like a criminal.

Reaching her apartment after a frenetic drive across London through rush-hour traffic, she left her mail unopened on a side table along with her bag and briefcase. Always so careful with her clothes, she shrugged her jacket from her shoulders and let it fall to the floor in bleak indifference. She kicked off her high-heeled shoes where she stood. She wandered to the window and stared at the skyline she loved without a scrap of interest in the gleam of the river between the houses, the sparrows on the roof, the glinting gold cross on the church spire just down the road.

She couldn't be bothered to cook, and she wasn't hungry, anyway. She changed into an orange tracksuit and curled up on the sofa in front of the TV with a pot of tea and a sandwich on a tray. But she didn't take in a single word or scene of the programme she only switched on to fill the silence that weighed so heavily.

The silent telephone mocked a loneliness she had never realised. She didn't want to think about the loneliness of her life in the future. She didn't want to think about the upheaval in her life since she had taken up her appointment as junior registrar with the CSU— or Tyler, the cause of it all. It was too painful. But snatches of things he had said, glimpses of the way he had looked and smiled, kept coming into her mind along with the memory of that first kiss on her first day at Sandy's.

A stranger's kiss that had been so familiar, so welcome, that it seemed she had waited all her life for it and recognised her destiny as his strong arms went round her and he took possession of her lips—and her heart.

She had stupidly believed Tyler felt just as she did. But all those weeks of encouraging her to love him and trust him, of coaxing her to wonder if marriage and career could be combined—it had all meant nothing, after all. Just like her amoral and totally heartless sister, Tyler treated love like a game—and he'd won, hadn't he? He'd got her into bed, with her wanton, willing co-operation, which proved that she and Van were much more alike than she had ever wanted to believe.

Now, having no reason to doubt Van's claim that he had asked her to marry him, Venetia knew she would never again hear his deep, disturbing voice murmuring *sweetheart* as if he meant it, never again know the warm caress of his hand or the hardness of his lean body as it swept her to paradise.

It shamed her that she still wanted him so desperately. She hugged her aching breasts and rocked to and fro in an agony of love and longing—and almost jumped out of her skin as the sudden, unnerving shrill of the doorbell cut across the unheeded voice of a popular comedian and the canned laughter of an unseen audience.

She was tempted to ignore the summons, in no mood for visitors. The bell rang again, an impatient double ring. With a sigh, Venetia unfurled herself from the sofa, drying the tears on her face with her hands like a child as she went to open the door to her unexpected caller.

'Why the devil don't you answer your phone?' With that unceremonious greeting, Tyler hobbled past her into the apartment, uninvited but never doubting that he was welcome.

'It hasn't rung.' She stared at him with unbelieving eyes.

He had slit the seam of a trouser leg to accommodate the plastered foot and managed to struggle into a loose summer shirt. His jet hair was rumpled and he looked angry, harassed. Venetia found it hard to grasp that he was actually here, in her apartment, where she had so often imagined him. A very potent presence, alarming, exciting—and utterly astonishing.

'I've been ringing you for nearly two hours!' Limping across to the bright red instrument on the bureau, Tyler frowned at the number on its dial and compared it with a piece of paper from his pocket. 'You're ex-directory, or I'd have discovered a lot sooner that I've got the wrong number. Two numbers transposed, in fact. Took it down in a hurry, I guess. No wonder I've never been able to contact you at home. . .'

He flopped on to the sofa, looking so weary, so vulnerable, that Venetia had to lock her hands together to keep from reaching out to him.

'I'm not sure what you're doing here. . .what you want,' she said uncertainly, struggling with a most undignified impulse to launch herself into his arms and sob out her relief against his welcoming chest.

She mustn't jump to conclusions. It wasn't likely that he was here because he couldn't keep away, as her foolish heart hoped. There could be any number of reasons why he'd come halfway across London to see her. A desire to marry her sister was right at the top of the list.

'I want a number of things. But first and foremost, I want this nonsense about you and Linnie stamped on the head,' he told her bluntly. 'I must have been told by ten different people this afternoon that you're about to marry the man!'

He was so angry that Venetia saw the tremble of his powerful body, the throb of a pulse in the lean jaw and the effort it took him to control the towering rage of his emotions. The shock of his words reverberated through her own slender frame, but she realised instantly what had happened. Sister Merridew *had* repeated that idiotic remark, and the gossips had obviously had a field day ever since!

'You've heard about that,' she said ruefully.

'It's all over Sandy's! Why on earth did you allow such nonsense to get a hold? I might have believed it, but I ran into Van when I was trying to locate you. She was foaming at the mouth—and who could blame her? But, as I pointed out, it was an easy mistake for people to make, in the circumstances. After all, I've suffered myself from confusing the two of you!'

'What mistake?' Venetia was thoroughly bewildered.

Tyler leaned his dark head against the back of the sofa, calmer now after the seemingly interminable taxi journey across the city, soothed by the sight of the slim girl in her bright tracksuit, her glorious hair billowing about her pale, startled face. 'He can't be engaged to both of you, can he?'

Venetia floundered in a sea of confusion. 'I really don't know what you're talking about, Tyler.'

He frowned. 'But Van said she'd told you.'

She sat down on the arm of the sofa, abruptly, her legs suddenly too weak and wobbly to support her. 'She did—but I didn't realise she was talking about *Rogan*. Ever since I heard that she was in the car with you when you had your accident. . .'

'For goodness' sake, I was only giving her a lift home from the hospital—I saw her in the car park as I came out. Is that why you were so frosty on the phone earlier?' Tyler's tone of amazement was patently sincere, and Venetia wanted to laugh out loud with relief. She wanted to cry. Suddenly, everything was crystal

clear. She and Van had been talking at cross-purposes
on the stairs that evening. It was Rogan and not Tyler
that her sister had decided she wanted and must have,
come hell or high water—and *oh*, how she wished them
happiness!

Especially now, when the man she loved with all her
singing heart seemed to be saying with the burning in
those dark eyes that he loved her too!

'Is it such a blow? Have I got it all wrong?' Tyler
demanded brusquely, confused in his turn, suddenly
unsure.

Unused to being brushed off so decisively, puzzled
by her change of heart when things had been going so
well, he had rushed to Sandy's to confront her, only to
be greeted by the news that she was engaged to his
boss.

He'd been stunned—and then, remembering her
sweetness, her shy and touching response to his lovemaking, he'd known in his bones, in his blood, deep in
the heart of him, that a girl like Venetia didn't tumble
into bed with any man unless she loved him. It hadn't
been conceit but a certainty that had lifted his spirits
and eased his troubled mind and heart. Now Tyler
couldn't bear to think that perhaps he had completely
mistaken the matter and that she really did love the
man who seemed to play such an important part in her
life.

Venetia slowly slid to the cushion at his side. 'I think
we might both be on the verge of getting it all right at
last,' she said softly, smiling at him.

Relief swept over him as he saw the warm reassurance in the beautiful violet eyes. He reached for her
thankfully. 'I never want to go through anything like

the last few hours again,' he said fervently. 'I knew it had to be a mistake, but I needed to hear it from you.' He drew her close. 'I love you so much, sweetheart. If you're planning to marry anyone then it's got to be *me*.'

She nestled happily into his arms. 'If you insist,' she said demurely.

Tyler brushed the cloud of golden hair from her face and looked deep into the lovely, luminous depths of the eyes that held no more secrets from him. 'I do. I've never felt like this about anyone. You're all I've ever wanted in a woman. I want you with me for the rest of my life. Haven't I been telling you for weeks that destiny meant us to be together?'

Venetia curved a hand about his lean cheek with loving tenderness. 'I think you might be right about destiny,' she murmured, and kissed him, her heart welling with love for him.

Maybe it was a little soon to be so sure that they were meant to spend the rest of their lives together. It wasn't too soon to be sure that she loved him with all her heart.

Venetia had known that from the very first kiss.

A special gift for Christmas

Four romantic stories by four of your favourite authors for you to unwrap and enjoy this Christmas.

Robyn Donald   STORM OVER PARADISE
Catherine George   BRAZILIAN ENCHANTMENT
Emma Goldrick   SMUGGLER'S LOVE
Penny Jordan   SECOND-BEST HUSBAND

Published on 11th October, 1991   Price: £6.40

Available from Boots, Martins, John Menzies, W.H. Smith, and other paperback stockists.

Also available from Mills and Boon Reader Service, P.O. Box 236, Thornton Road, Croydon, Surrey CR9 3RU.

—MEDICAL ♥ ROMANCE—

The books for your enjoyment this month are:

A SPECIAL CHALLENGE Judith Ansell
HEART IN CRISIS Lynne Collins
DOCTOR TO THE RESCUE Patricia Robertson
BASE PRINCIPLES Sheila Danton

♥　♥　♥　♥　♥

Treats in store!

Watch next month for the following absorbing stories:

MEDICAL DECISIONS Lisa Cooper
DEADLINE LOVE Judith Worthy
NO TIME FOR ROMANCE Kathleen Farrell
RELATIVE ETHICS Caroline Anderson